Brady: Encouraged to Heal

The Barnabas Chronicles
Book 5

By

Ronna M. Bacon

Exodus 15:26

If you diligently heed the voice of the Lord your God and do what is right in His sight, give ear to His commandments and keep all His statutes, I will put none of the diseases on you which I have brought on the Egyptians. For I am the Lord who heals you. NKJV

Table of Contents

Chapter 1

Drawing in a deep breath of fresh air, Brady Coghlan stood for a moment, his eyes on the distance hill he could see through the trees and underbrush. This was what he needed, he thought, to be away from everyone, to be on his own. Brady had gone to his employer and friend, Barnabas Carey of The Barnabas Foundation, asking for some time. It had been a rough few months in his work as a paramedic, to say nothing of the assaults and abduction and whatnot that his four friends had just gone through, even though they had found their ladies to love and adore in that all.

He was beaten up, beaten down, and soul weary. Almost losing his friend, Bradon, to a drowning and Bradon's lady, Ennis, to a knife attack, he felt the need to walk away, to be refreshed, to spend some time healing in God's presence. Barnabas had taken one look at him and nodded, just asking that he keep in touch, and how much time did he need?

Brady had taken a leave of two weeks from his work as a paramedic, knowing he would be covered. That's what his friends on the EMS teams did. He didn't know if he would be able to continue, but he would sort that out, he prayed, over the next couple of weeks.

Coming to a sudden halt, he searched the area he was in, trying to find the source of the stench. He recognized it only too well. Over the course of the years he had been a paramedic, they had had calls to places where corpses were found, even though there was nothing they could do. He hated that part of his work, knowing someone was dead and he couldn't help them. He saw the pile of clothing and groaned. Not what he needed to be finding on his vacation.

Backing away, Brady reached for his phone, hoping he had service. He wasn't quite sure of the location, but gave it as best he could to the dispatcher, who seemed to know where he was.

Two hours later, Brady stood, leaning against a police cruiser, arms crossed against his chest, watching the activity that surrounded the area. He knew the coroner was on the scene, but he frowned as he studied the older man, wondering why the delay, why they weren't moving the body. He shrugged.

The police officer approached Brady carefully, not sure of the man standing in front of him. He had asked for information on him, surprised to find out who his employer was. It still didn't explain why he was out in the wild of Northern Ontario.

"Mr. Coghlan?"

Brady turned as the officer spoke. "It's Brady. Do you have all you need from me?"

The officer nodded. "I do, but I would ask that you stay in the area for now, in case we have more questions." He looked down at his notes. "You're not from here."

"No, I'm not. I'm from Nova Scotia but have lived in Southern Ontario, near Lake Erie, for years." Brady sighed. "If I can't leave, I guess I'll be needing to find somewhere to stay."

The officer grinned. "I'm Eric Thomas. I know where you can stay. My aunt has a B&B and I'm sure she'll find a room for you."

Brady nodded, his black hair reflecting blue highlights in the sun, his deep gray eyes watchful.

"That sounds good. How soon can I leave? My truck's in the parking lot down below."

Eric grinned. "We know it is and right now, it's blocked in. If you can leave your keys, I'll have it brought to you." He took Bradon's keys even as he glanced down at his watch. "I'm about finished here and can give you a lift."

Brady's eyes lifted as he heard the sound of a vehicle and saw a small white van stop and then the door opening. He frowned as he studied the young woman who dropped from the seat and walked around to open the side door. He watched as she pulled on the white coveralls and a mask, picked up booties and her kits and walked towards the coroner, who had approached her.

Eric shook his head. "I thought Dan would call in Fynn. It's not a nice line of work she's in." He pointed to the trail. "Let's head out. I have to stop by the detachment and then I can take you to my aunt's. I'm sorry you can't take your truck."

Two hours later, Brady sat in a local diner with Eric and some of Eric's friends. He listened to their talk, but wondered at the empty chair next to him. Eric sat on the other side of it, his arm laying across the back as he waited for their food.

Brady jumped as he felt a hand touch his shoulder before the chair beside him slid back and the young lady he had seen in the woods sat beside him, her head shaking at something Eric had asked in a quiet voice. Eric looked past her and then introduced her.

"Brady? This is Fynn Daley. She's the one that was out there today." He paused, knowing Fynn was always hesitant to give her occupation.

Fynn turned, her curious aqua eyes with the flecks of green, blue and brown focusing on him.

"Hi." Her voice was quiet, her gaze assessing in a professional manner. "You're the one?"

"The one?" He studied her, thinking that her short cap of curls reminded him of the copper pots his grandmother had had.

"The one who found the body."

"That would be me." He wondered that she didn't say or ask anything more, just turning to answer a question from Eric.

Later, he walked beside her as she headed for the sidewalk, obviously not having a vehicle.

"Wait? You're walking?" Brady's hand on her arm stopped her.

"I am. I usually walk when I can." She paused, her eyes raised to his, thinking how tall he was, six four likely. She found it odd having to look up at a man, being tall for a woman herself.

"Let me give you a lift." He grinned, the grin lighting up his face. "I just can't let a lady walk on her own."

She snorted, causing him to stare at her, and then laugh. "My friends know better."

"Well, then, consider me a friend who won't let a friend out on her own."

She shook her head again. "I go into places most men wouldn't go in to. I have to for my work."

Fynn turned as she heard running footsteps approaching them, finding Brady shoving her behind him before he was tackled and taken down. A swift blow to his temple knocked him unconscious even as Fynn scrambled backwards, trying to find her feet to flee, unable to before her wrist was grasped and she was pulled away from Brady.

She fought her assailant, finally scraping her fingernails across his face, bringing a cry of pain from him before she was shoved violently to the ground, her face scraping in the gravel. The man knelt with a knee in her back, his mouth close to her ear.

"Don't go any further with your investigation. Let it drop."

"I can't do that."

"Do it and you live. Don't and you die. And he dies too." A hard shove from the knee drove the breath from her before she heard running footsteps heading away from her and then footsteps running towards them.

Eric reached to help her up, frowning at her face, before he questioned her.

"Who was that?"

"I have no idea, Eric. Other than I was told to drop the investigation from today, or I died and so would Brady." She stalked towards Brady, who by this time was sitting up, being assessed by a paramedic friend of Eric's. "Just who are you?"

He looked up, pain flickering across his face. "What do you mean? Just who am I? I am a paramedic from southern Ontario. I work for The Barnabas Foundation. I have never been here before and I have no idea who I found." He glared at her, not seeing the amused looks on the men around them. "And just what do you do, anyway?"

"I'm a forensic entomologist. And why would I be told to drop the case or we both died? Who did you anger?"

"Me?" Brady shot to his feet, a hand to his head as it throbbed with pain. "I didn't anger anyone. Did you?"

Fynn shot him a dark look before she spun on her heel and stalked away, leaving Brady to stare after her, the men around him trying to hide their smiles.

Chapter 2

The next day, Brady wandered the town he found himself in, not willing to move on, not willing to stay. Eric had contacted him that morning and told him that he was free to move on if he wanted to, but there was an underlying tone of humour in his voice that Brady didn't understand. He finally settled himself into a booth at the diner where he had eaten at the night before, reaching for the menu, and then just laying it down, tapping at it idly. Having no idea why he was so restless, Brady sighed. He needed to go home but didn't want to.

Hearing footsteps stop beside him, he glanced up and then slid from the booth, staring at Fynn as she stood there, hesitant to disturb him, his eyes finding Eric right behind her.

"Fynn?"

"Brady, I need to apologize for last night." She slid into the seat he had risen from, Eric sliding into the one across from her.

Brady frowned at Eric for a moment, who just grinned at him, and then slid down beside Fynn, watching as she played with the menu he had just sat down on the tabletop. His hand finally reached to still hers, bringing her eyes up to him. She's haunted by something, isn't she, Lord? And how do I help her?

"Who scared you, Fynn?"

She stared at him, disbelief on her face, but knowledge in her eyes that he was right. "I'm not sure what you mean." She waved at the waitress to place her order, avoiding Eric's frown and look and certainly not looking at Brady.

"I repeat myself." Brady spoke after the waitress had moved away. "Who has scared you that badly? It's not just from last night."

Fynn once more avoided his eyes, finding Eric watching her closely, before her glance moved to the window. A shuttered look covered her face.

"That's okay, Fynn. I'm prying. I don't really need to know, but I will pray for you." His eyes were on his folded hands, not seeing when she turned her gaze to him. "It's just that I hate to see any lady afraid. The wives of four of my friends have gone through some pretty bad stuff. I've seen it on my job. So, again, if you don't mind my asking, who scared you?" At this point, he looked up, to find her watching him closely.

Fynn sighed. "I'm not sure, Brady. I have felt like I have been watched, followed, things have been moved around in the lab where I work." She shivered, not from cold, but from the fear that was growing within her.

"Have you reported this?"

She shook her head, hearing Eric's low murmur. "I'm sorry, Eric. I had no proof other than a gut feeling. I did take to my supervisor at work, and we've upped the security there, but someone is still getting in."

Eric nodded. "And without proof, you weren't sure anyone would believe you. I get that, Fynn. But, please, tell me next time?"

She shook her head at her cousin. The only children in their family, they had grown up almost like siblings, fighting with one another but having each other's backs as needed. "I can't promise that, Eric. I just can't."

Brady moved his arms back for the plates to be set down in front of them, staring down at his own meal, hearing Eric ask the blessing on their food, and then the two cousins talking quietly. He was searching through his memories to see what he could offer her, and then sighed to himself. He wasn't close enough to do that. He just wanted to make it better for her, and knew the thirteen others who lived in his building would want the same.

Fynn laid her hand on Brady's arm, causing him to look up at her, a frown on his face that disappeared as he studied her. This is a lady I would like to get to know better, Lord, but I just don't see how that's possible. I don't want to move from where I am. It's too much of a home for me, and the guys and their ladies are family. And she has work here that she won't leave.

Fynn stood later that day, her eyes on her work, but her mind on Brady. What was it about him that made her feel safe and cherished, Lord? Is he the one I've been praying for, the one who will help me solve what's happening? Is he the one that I'm missing in my heart? I've hurt so much for years that I just don't know where to begin to heal. She sighed, reaching for one of the vials in front of her, no longer so eager to press ahead in her line of work. What is causing this discontent, Lord?

Chapter 3

A week later, Fynn stared at the vials and containers on the lab desk, her mind once more wandering to Brady. They had spent time together over the last week, and she had to admit, he was wriggling his way into her heart. She despaired of what she would do when he left the next day. Brady had sighed as he told her that, that he had to head home, but he really didn't want to leave her here when she was facing something

She studied her work, knowing she had just finished the task from the previous week and at the moment, had nothing pending. A growing conviction and desire in her heart had her looking up, before nodding. She hung up her lab coat, threw away her gloves, and headed for her supervisor, letter in hand. Fynn had prayed hard about her decision and knew she was making the right one. She just didn't know how her parents would react, but she didn't think it would matter too much to them. She had always felt an outsider in her home, but welcomed at Eric's. She wondered at that.

Her supervisor stared at her and then at the letter of resignation in his hand, not sure if Fynn was really quitting.

"Fynn?"

"I am sorry, Joe. I just can't do this anymore. I need a break." She paused, biting at her lip. "I have everything up to date. Nothing is outstanding or pending. I have never taken holidays except for the odd day here and there. With my accrued vacation and sick time, this brings it well past the time I have set for my resignation."

Joe sighed, knowing he had lost the best one in his office. "Okay, then, I guess. You will be missed." He peered closely at her, seeing the fine lines that were beginning to show. "If you change your mind?

She simply shook her head and walked away, finding a box to pack her personal belongings from her office, noting that she really didn't have that much. Her pass and keys were handed off to the security guard, who stared at her in disbelief, and then she walked to her car, placing the box into the trunk, and then just standing, her hand on the trunk lid, blinking back tears as she realized that she had just cut her ties with her family, her friends, and her work. Where now, Lord?

Brady watched her closely as she stood in front of him, not looking at him. They had spent a lot of time together during the last week, and he cherished the friendship that she offered him. Eric had taken him to one side, told him that she didn't offer friendship that freely, and he was to make sure he didn't hurt her. Brady had nodded, his eyes watching Fynn from where he stood, and sighed to himself, thinking that was exactly what he would be doing.

Fynn stood, hesitation in her that was not normal, before she looked up at Brady, taking the hand he reached out for her. These two had had deep conversations over the last week, finding out how much they thought alike, but also had had spirited discussions.

"Fynn?" Brady's voice had held concern as they walked along the riverside paths.

"I don't know if I made a right decision today, Brady." She sighed, worry niggling at her mind. She no longer had employment, but maybe, just maybe, she thought, she could make a break from here.

"And that would be?" Brady's voice held confidence in her decision.

"I quit my job. I am now at loose ends." She looked up again, seeing his eyes watching her as he stopped their steps.

"You did? Okay. So, now where do you go?'

She shrugged. "I have no idea. I'm thinking of leaving town."

Brady turned as he heard running footsteps and swept Fynn into his arms, pulling her away from the area. "Where can we go, Fynn?"

She looked around. "No where. This is a dead end area of the path." She spun to face the man standing in front of her. "You again? What part of I don't know what you want is it that you can't understand?"

The man gave a twisted smile, evil showing in his eyes, as he studied her before he looked up at Brady. "You know what I want. Drop the case."

Fynn snorted. "I don't have any cases and I certainly wouldn't drop on your say so. So, get lost." She looked past him, not seeing his sudden charge towards her, taking her to the ground, Brady hitting the area beside her, before the man was up and away.

Brady lay still for a moment, his head turning to watch Fynn, before he sat up, reaching to help her to a sitting position, before he just wrapped her into his arms and held her. Eric stood for a moment, watching them. He had been following the man, determined to stop him from attacking Fynn again, but had lost sight of him. That was, until he heard Fynn's voice raised in anger..

Brady raised his eyes to look at Eric before shaking his head. Fynn was distraught, to say the least, and he hated that for her. Eric nodded and then headed past them, searching for their assailant, but knowing he would not find him. He stood, drawing in a deep breath, his eyes raised to the sky. This is it, isn't it, Lord? My best friend and almost sister is moving away. Sadness wafted through his heart. He could not keep, would not keep her here, not if she needed to move on. And it certainly seemed that way. Maybe, he thought, just maybe if she leaves town, this will stop, but he had no guarantees that it would.

Fynn finally raised her head and then stood, embarrassed for a moment, before she spun, her mouth opening to speak. Brady just shook his head and reached to wrap her into a hug. He didn't say anything for a moment.

"Where were you thinking of moving to?" He felt her shrug. "Would you consider moving my way?"

Fynn tilted her head back to look up at him. "I might. But you've never really told me about this foundation you work for."

Brady shook his head, his eyes on Eric heading their way. "Why don't we go find somewhere we can get a coffee. Eric looks as if he wants to talk to you too."

She looked over at her cousin, seeing the realization in his eyes that she was moving and sighed. This was not how she meant to do this. She felt her phone vibrating and from force of habit, pulled it up, checking the text message. She paled as she read it, causing the two men to exchange a glance before Eric reached for her phone. His face grew stern as he read it.

"Fynn? Your home?"

She nodded, tears near the surface. "Someone broke into it. I can't do this, Eric. I just can't."

Chapter 4

Brady watched Fynn closely as she moved through her house later that night, picking things up, putting them back down, moving aimlessly, he thought. He finally approached her, hands on her arms to stop her, causing her to raise her eyes to him.

"Fynn? What is it you really want to do? Stay here tonight? Go to the B&B?" He watched her face shift with her thoughts.

"What do I really want to do? Leave town? Right at this moment." She shrugged away from him, disturbed that he had been able to read her so well. Lord, where do I go? I feel anchorless right now.

"Then, move my way. I'm sure you could find work or even set up your own business, if that's what you want. I know Barnabas would help. That's what they do."

Fynn spun at his words, hope on her face for the first time in days, he thought. "He'd do that?"

"More than likely. If he won't fund you, then he knows plenty of people who will."

She walked back towards him. "Okay. So. He would?"

Brady laughed, his phone out, sending off a text to Barnabas. "I'll ask him. I don't think I explained how we work. Each one of the guys is employed by the Foundation, who pay their wages, but we work for different employers in town. This way, they can hire as they need to without feeling the pinch of finding extra cash to do so. We also volunteer our time to different organizations."

Fynn stood her mouth open in surprise, not seeing Eric standing behind her. "How can he do that?"

"Relax, Fynn. The Foundation is worth a lot of money, more than Barnabas or his father could ever spend. They do a lot with just the interest from the money." He felt his phone vibrate and looking down, saw Barnabas was calling him. He excused himself to take the call.

"Brady?" Barnabas' voice held concern. "I got your text. What's up?"

"Barnabas, I didn't expect you to call back so soon."

"Branigan was here, asking about you. Can I put you on speaker? That way, we can all be part of the discussion."

"Yeah. Sure. I guess."

"Okay, tell me about this." Brady could hear the creak in Barnabas' chair and knew he was sitting back, his elbows on the arms of the chair, head tilted as he listened.

"Fynn Daley is a forensics entomologist. I met her when I found that body. She has been attacked twice in the last week, being ordered to stop her investigation. She has no idea what that would be. She has also indicated that she thinks her lab and office have been searched." Brady paused, turning so he could watch her and Eric as they picked up the pieces of her life that had been strewn around the living room. "Her home was broken into tonight and tossed. She has also quit her job here. Fynn wants to move away. What can we do to help her?"

Branigan and Barnabas exchanged glances. They could hear the same tone in his voice that the other four had had when their ladies were going through things. They just shook their heads.

"If she's quit her work, where is she planning on living?" Barnabas had a good guess as to where Brady would like her.

"I have no idea." Brady had turned away for a moment and the turned back to watch Fynn and Eric as they stood, her eyes on Brady, Eric watching Fynn. "She seems to be wanting to leave this area."

"If she does and wants to head this way, I'll talk to her." Barnabas asked a few more questions, some that Brady could answer and some that he couldn't.

Fynn studied him as he pocketed his phone, standing for a moment staring into space, before his eyes turned to her. Brady walked towards her, stopping just short of her, his head ducking so he could stare at her face before he looked past her at Eric, seeing how torn he was for his cousin.

"Brady?" Fynn's voice was hopeful, but her heart was heavy. She just didn't think anyone would help her out. They hadn't in the past when she had needed someone. Well, other than Eric, and he didn't know the full reason she had chosen her profession.

"Barnabas asked where you were planning on moving to." He watched carefully as she stared at him before turning to Eric.

"I don't know, Brady. I just don't know. I can't stay here. But if I move, does he follow me?"

Eric spoke from behind her as he wrapped her into a hug, pulling her back against him.

"Don't let fear rule your life, cuz. If you need to move on, move on. It's not like you can't." He paused, biting at his lip before he continued. "I know your parents do love you, but they are just so complete in one another, you have taken the backseat all these years. Mom has mentioned that on more than one occasion."

She nodded. "I know." Her voice was sad but resigned. "I know that, Eric." She turned to look at him. "I just don't like leaving you. You're more than a cousin. You're my big brother."

Eric smiled. "As you are my sister. But God has opened this door so unexpectedly for you." He paused, biting at his lip. "Besides, I'm moving as well."

"You are?"

Eric nodded. "I am. I have found a little town on Lake Erie that needs an investigator. I didn't want to tell you, but it seems we're heading in the same direction."

Brady had been watching, his eyes narrowing before he nodded. He knew the town. It was Bradon's wife's, Ennis', town. That was good. It was close to the Foundation Building where he lived and where he hoped Fynn would take up residence, at least for a while.

Chapter 5

Standing outside Fynn's home early the next morning, listening as the early morning chatter of nature was starting, Brady looked around, a frown on his face. He sensed someone out there, just couldn't see anyone. It wasn't light enough, he thought. He turned back as he heard footsteps approaching.

Fynn studied the man in front of her for a moment, wondering why she trusted him so quickly. It must be a God thing, she thought, something her aunt always had her looking for. She watched as his smile lit up for her and he reached for the bags she had in her hand, quickly stuffing them into the back seat of his truck, and then opening the door for her, a hand out to help her up to the seat.

Brady waited as she did up her seatbelt before he closed the door, watching her for a moment before he walked around and slide behind the wheel, his fingers tapping quietly on it before he started the truck, and then surprised her by reaching for her hand.

"I always pray before I travel, Fynn." He watched the relief that flooded her face

"Do you? So do I. I don't know of many others who do, except for Eric and his parents."

"Where is Eric this morning? I thought he would be here."

"He was. He was headed into work. I wouldn't let him stay long." Fynn stared out the window at her hometown, watching a familiar buildings and scenes passed by, knowing she would never move back here, if she ever even came to visit, she thought.

Four hours later, Brady pulled off the road into a little eating area, his eyes searching. He felt followed but he couldn't see what vehicle. He turned to Fynn, a smile on his face as he watched her sleeping, reaching behind him for a pillow he tucked under her head, and then a blanket he tucked around her, his hand lingering for a few seconds on her face. His heart raised in prayer for his new friend, knowing already he didn't want her to disappear.

She's the one, isn't she, Lord? Is she the one who is my helpmeet, the other half to my heart, my cherished one? He turned back to stare out of the windshield, his thoughts muddled for a change, before he shook his head and pulled back on to the highway. There were still miles to go, he thought. I will be glad to be home.

Fynn had stirred slightly as she felt Brady's hand on her face and then drifted back to sleep, her mind not active for a change, she thought. Usually she couldn't sleep, her mind too active. What was it about Brady that calmed her enough that she could?

Brady finally pulled to a stop in his town, jumping down from the truck, and stretching. He needed a break before he drove the last few miles to home. Turning, he watched as Fynn still slept and wondered if she would even sleep that night. Lord, heal my lady. Bring strength to her. I fear we are just starting something, like the other four guys. I don't want to see her go through what they did, particularly Ennis. Bradon almost lost her that day, Lord. I can see how he watches her at times, when he knows she's not aware of it.

Returning to the truck with the few fresh groceries he knew he needed and some for Fynn as well, Brady stood for a moment, feeling a prickling in the back of his neck. Someone had followed them, that much he knew. But he also knew he would never see them. Not unless they wanted him to and he doubted that very much.

He turned on to the highway leading towards his home. It was late afternoon, and he was tired. Brady twisted his neck to relieve some tension, and then looked in horror at the truck racing his way, in his lane. He twisted the wheel to go around it but the truck moved back towards him. Lord, where do I go?

He spun the wheel to turn the truck back into his own lane, his heart in his mouth as the tires hit the gravel and then his control was gone. He could only hold on and pray they both survived the crash. His head hit the window and as his consciousness faded, he prayed for safety for Fynn, not for himself. Brady didn't hear the scream that came from Fynn as she roused and saw the ground rushing towards her as the truck rolled, before landing back on its wheels, dust sifting through the air as silence once more reigned.

The creatures that had fled at the noise and at the large object heading their way finally made their paths back out, standing to stare at the truck before moving on. They scattered once more as they heard and saw the truck that suddenly stopped and the doors on it popping open, to let two men out who ran for Brady's vehicle.

Chapter 6

Branigan Clery and Brennen Connolly had been in town earlier, heading home not long after Brady had left town. Their conversation was quiet, sparked with laughter, before Brennen frowned.

"Branigan, those look like skid marks."

Branigan agreed, his foot easing off the accelerator even as his eyes searched the area. "Whoever it was hit the gravel. Do you see anyone?"

Brennen was searching and then pointed. "There. Oh no!"

Branigan shot him a glance and then turned his eyes to the truck. "Brady?"

"I think so." Brennen barely waited for Branigan to stop the vehicle before he was out and racing for the truck, Branigan on his heels.

Brennen tugged hard at Brady's door, then leaned in to the window, his hands framing his face. "It's Brady, but he's not alone." He looked around at Branigan. "I can't get this door open." He reached for the back door, with the same results.

"He's rolled it at least once." Branigan ran for the passenger side. "Call it in, Brennen. This is not Brady, to do this."

"No, it's not." His phone in his hand, Brennen ran for Branigan's truck, searching for the tire iron and returning with it. "They're on their way. Ten minutes or less." He looked down at the tire iron and shook his head. "This isn't going to work."

Branigan shot him a glance and then agreed. "The frame is jammed. I can't get this door open either." He looked up as he heard a vehicle. "There's Barnabas?"

Brennen was off, stopping to drop the tire iron back into the truck before he ran towards Barnabas.

"Brennen? Is that Brady?" Barnabas ran towards the truck even as he heard the sounds of sirens rising and falling as they approached.

"It is. He's rolled it. I'm not sure how, though." Brennen slid to a stop, a hand out to stop Barnabas just short of the truck. "He has a lady with him. Do you know anything about that?"

Barnabas nodded, his face grim as he assessed the truck. "Did he hit the gravel?"

Branigan nodded. "It looks like it. But I can't figure out how."

"His dash camera may help." Barnabas stepped back as he watched the firefighters approaching, gear in hand. "What was that you said about a lady?"

"She's in the passenger seat." Branigan turned to stare at the truck. "What's that about?"

"Fynn." The two other men turned to stare at Barnabas. "Fynn Daley. She's moving this way. We talked to Brady late yesterday about her, Branigan. He sent me a text early this morning that she would be with him."

"That we did." Branigan turned to watch the activity around the truck, seeing the paramedics arriving. "Brady was due back at work on Monday."

"He was?" Barnabas turned away for a moment, hearing his name called. "Will? You're here?"

Will Peters, police chief in the nearby town that covered the area the Foundation Building was in, stood beside them, studying the scene.

"I heard it was Brady."

Barnabas nodded. "It is. He was almost home from his vacation. I am not sure what happened."

They looked towards the truck as they heard the screeching and groaning of the metal as the equipment pulled it away from the two in the cab, and then watched the hurried movements of the paramedics and firefighters as they worked to free the two.

The two working on Brady stood for a few seconds, their eyes on their friend, seeing him slumped forward against the seatbelt before they worked to stabilize him. A neck collar was in place before the older of the two slid into the back seat of the truck and steadied Brady as he was moved backwards. A quickly indrawn breath from the younger paramedic sounded loud in the silence.

Brady groaned, his eyes flickering as he woke, not sure what had happened or even where he was. Dried blood showed in a trickle below one nostril, and still dripped from a small cut over his eyebrow, down across his eyelid and cheek.

"Brady? Can you hear us?"

Another groan came from Brady as he answered, his voice gruff with pain. "I can, Travis. Where am I?"

"You're still in your truck. Looks like you rolled it somehow. Do you remember what happened?"

Brady shook his head, his face tightening in pain at the movement. "No, I don't. Am I home?"

"You are. You don't remember?"

"No, I don't." Brady's voice faded as he lost his grip on consciousness.

Travis shared a look with David before he shook his head, his attention going momentarily to the team working on Fynn.

"Let's get him out of here and to help. Doc's working today?"

"He is. He's on the afternoon shift. I'm glad." David reached for Brady, the hands helping gentle as they shifted him to a backboard and then to the stretcher, which was then wheeled hurriedly to the waiting ambulance. Travis stood for a moment, eyeing Brady, before he turned to watch the activity at the truck. Who did this, he wondered? Brady's too careful a driver to have this happen to. And I wonder who the lady is. He wasn't dating anyone when he left for vacation. He slammed the doors shut and then heading for the driver's seat, his mind running scenarios before he shook his head, at a loss to explain anything other than a good friend was hurt.

Chapter 7

The officer watching as the other paramedic team worked on Fynn took the wallet he was handed, his eyes on her before he opened it, a surprised look crossing his face.

"How is she?" His voice sounded loud in the sudden silence.

"Not sure. She's battered, that's for sure." Carol turned back to the other lady, reaching to undo the seatbelt, her partner, Ted, in the back seat, helping to stop Fynn for falling forward. They had found her slumped against the door.

The officer nodded, his eyes once more on the identification he held. He turned to study the truck and then walked towards Will, a puzzled look on his face.

Will reached for the wallet, assessing the look on the officer's face, before he looked down at the license.

"Fynn Daley?"

"Yes, sir. I thought she lived up north."

"She does. What is she doing here and with Brady?" He turned at a sound from Barnabas. "Barnabas, do you know why?"

Barnabas exchanged a look with his two friends before he nodded. "I do. Brady met her when he was up there on vacation. Long story short is that she was ready to move, on the run you might say, and he suggested she might like to move this way. Apparently she agreed. I knew they were heading this way. Just didn't expect this."

"I will need to talk to her employer." Will watched as Barnabas moved slightly. "Barnabas?"

Barnabas sighed. "She doesn't work there now. She resigned and decided to move this way. That's why she was with Brady."

"I see." Will handed the officer back Fynn's wallet. "Follow her in, Justin. I'll be by later." He watched as the paramedics settled Fynn onto a stretcher, did what they needed to and then wheeled it to the waiting ambulance, Justin following and then hopping up into the back, to settle into a corner where he could watch Fynn.

Justin was puzzled. He knew of Fynn's work, that as Dr. Fynn Daley, she was well known and respected in her field, even at her young age. He figured she must have hit college around age 16 and then graduated with her master's at age 20. He shook his head. There is no way he would have done that.

Doc Adams looked around as he heard his name called before his eyes dropped to the stretcher being wheeled towards him and gave an inaudible sound.

"Brady? Travis, what happened?" He walked quickly that way, pointing to an examination room, before he was at Brady's side, his eyes watchful, before he glanced up at Travis.

"Car accident. Somehow, he rolled his truck on the highway near your place."

"Rolled his truck? That's not Brady."

"No, it's not. He was awake for a few seconds. Didn't remember doing that."

Doc nodded, his hands already at work assessing his young friend. "Sue, we'll need imaging. Blood work." Doc paused for a moment, his face thoughtful, before he shook his head. He had a thought that just maybe Brady was going to go through what his other four young friends had, and that he feared. Each one had been through enough violence.

Brady stirred, the familiar odours of antiseptic and sickness in his nostrils. His eyes blinked open, and he stared around before he groaned. What did he do, he wondered?

"Brady? Can you look at me?" Doc's voice was soft but firm and Brady did just what he had been asked to do.

"Doc?"

"You were in an accident, Brady. No, don't move. You're not getting up yet." Doc's hand on Brady's chest kept him still. "Do you remember anything about the accident?"

"Accident? What accident?" Brady's eyes flickered open and closed, before he focused on Doc.

"You were in an accident. Do you remember?"

"No, I don't." He looked around almost in a frantic manner. "Fynn?"

"Fynn? Who's that?"

"She was with me. I need to find her. She's in danger." Brady pushed at Doc's hands and then the blankets, before his head fell back and he faded away from them.

Doc looked around as he heard footsteps and Will and Barnabas stood beside him.

"Has he been awake?" Will's voice was quiet as he spoke.

"He was. He was asking for a Fynn."

"Fynn Daley. She was with him." Barnabas shook his head. "Why Brady?"

"Who is this woman?"

"Dr. Fynn Daley. She's a forensic entomologist. Apparently, Brady convinced her to move this way."

"He did? That doesn't sound like our Brady." Doc eyed the two men before he shook his head. "Don't tell me. He's set for an adventure just like the other four."

"Looks that way. How is he, Doc?" Barnabas was concerned enough that he didn't leave when the stretcher bearing Brady was taken to the imaging department.

"We'll know more when I see the scans, but I don't think there's much damage done. He'll be bruised and sore. The cut on his forehead is minor. It won't need stitches. It's a concussion I'm worried about."

Chapter 8

Her head turning restlessly, Fynn roused in the early morning hours, her eyes opening. She groaned softly, her hand raising to feel at the side of her head. It hurt, she decided, and I have no idea why. And why am I in a hospital bed? She reached for the controls, raising the head of the bed, and then settling back, feeling better that she was sitting more upright. She hated lying flat on her back, always had. Lord, I don't remember where I am, but I don't think I'm at home. I know You're here, but I'm scared. I hurt in more ways than one, not just physical. I need to heal, Lord, but I have no idea just how to do that.

Her eyes slid closed as she listened to the quiet sounds of the late night hospital activity. She heard the soft tread of rubber-soled feet as they approached her bed and just kept from jumping in fear as a hand touched her wrist, feeling for a pulse and then the stethoscope as it was placed for the physician to listen to her heart. She heard the quiet words spoken and breathed a sigh of relief. No real damage, she thought. Just bumps. And bruises. A lump on her head that hurt. She wanted to touch it but didn't want whoever was in the room with her to know she was awake. Fynn listened as the steps moved away from her before she cracked open one eye and then popped open the other one.

Where is Brady, she questioned? Is he okay or even alive? Fynn pushed at the blankets and sat up, waiting for the spinning in her head to stop. What had happened? She knew the truck had rolled. She remembered the sight of the ground outside her window. It didn't seem like Brady to have done that, she thought. Her feet hit the floor and she moved towards the cupboard, finding her clothes and then heading for the bathroom, dressing quickly, the hospital gown abandoned on the floor. Her purse over her shoulder, she crept out of the door and then searched, finding Brady sitting in the waiting room, head back, eyes closed.

Brady had awakened not long before that, on his feet and dressed, heading for where he would find Fynn. He had already made an excursion her way that night, finding her sleeping, and being sent back to his own bed by the charge nurse, who frowned at him, but had smiled to herself at Brady's actions. Brady was well liked by the hospital staff, having won a place in their hearts by his compassion and caring for not only his patients but for everyone he met. She shook her head and walked back to the desk, her mind already on the multitude of tasks she had to perform that day.

He jumped as he felt a hand touch his before it gently touched his face. His eyes opened and he studied Fynn who sat beside him.

"Brady?"

"I'm okay, Fynn. Shaken. Battered." He watched as her eyes closed and a single tear crept down her cheek before his finger was on it, wiping it away.

"I'm so glad. I was scared."

Her admission told him much. He knew she went into areas most people would not. For her to admit she was scared both worried and touched him.

"Fynn? You're okay?"

"I am." She looked around, shivering with fear as she did so. "Can we leave?"

Brady grinned at her. "You want to leave this establishment?" He looked up and past her as he heard footsteps. "We do have a ride. Fynn, this is a friend of mine. Baird? What are you doing here?"

"Doc sent me. He figured you two would be making a break for it about this time." He grinned. "It's good to finally meet you, Fynn. Let's go before we're stopped." Baird looked up as he felt eyes on him and nodded at the charge nurse, who simply smiled and nodded.

Fynn frowned at him, not sure what he meant, before she turned to Brady, finding him watching her, a look on his face that gave her pause, but almost made her feel loved and cherished.

"All set?" Brady stood, hesitating as his head cleared before he wrapped a hand around Fynn's and led her down the stairs and out of the Emergency entrance. "Where are you parked, Baird? And just how did you get chosen?"

Baird just grinned as he pointed towards his vehicle. "Over there. Doc didn't say. He just walked up to me last night, asked me to be here about this time as he just knew you two would be making a break for it, as he put it."

"We can't just walk away!" Fynn dug in her heels, refusing to move forward. "We don't have our discharge papers." Her mouth opened as Baird held up a folder. "No way! That can't be them!"

"It is, Fynn." Brady almost shoved her into the truck and then slid in beside her. "Buckle up. Doc would have made arrangements for this. He knows me well."

She stared at him and then at Baird, who was nodding.

"Four of us have gone through stuff, Fynn. We have an infirmary in the building. Well stocked, I might add. I know. I spent time in it not too long ago."

"You did? Why?" Fynn's curiosity was getting the better of her.

"Let's just say I had an adventure and was hurt. The guys found me and also Berneen, my wife, and brought us to safety. Someday, we'll tell you our story."

Fynn frowned at him, disgruntled that he didn't say more. "I'll hold you to that. Later today will be our talk." Her eyes closed and her head went down on Brady's shoulder as she slept. He watched her for a moment, before his eyes raised, staring out the side window, not catching Baird's look at him.

Fynn stared around the suite she had just been ushered into, remembering to snap her mouth closed.

"Brady? This can't be right. It's too nice for a guest suite."

"It's not a guest suite. It's a regular everyday apartment and for you, yours to use. Barnabas had your belongings brought here when they cleaned out my truck. I'm just across the hall from you."

She shook her head. "This is too nice for me. I'm not used to that."

Baird studied her, seeing the fear, no terror, he thought, underlying her words and actions. He then studied Brady, noting that he had seen the same things and sighed. Knowing Brady, he will want to step in and make it all better, just like we all do. This time, I don't know that he can. Lord, please. Protect his heart. Protect Fynn's heart. Heal her from whatever it is she is running from. Lead her to run to You.

Baird stepped away quietly, moving back towards his own apartment. All the men had a suite in the building, with offices for each one on the main floor. Doc Adams and his wife, Anna, also had an apartment on the main floor, beside Barnabas.

Berneen looked up as Baird entered, before moving into his hug.

"They're home?"

"They are. Both are hurting, I can tell you that much."

"What's she like?" Berneen leaned back to watch her husband's face.

"Different. She's hurting, love. Really hurting. And running. Why, I don't know." He sighed. "She's young, Berneen. I would say a bit younger than you."

"How can that be?" Berneen was puzzled.

"She hit college at age 16, or university rather. She graduated with her doctorate degree at age 20 and went right to work. She needs a break but I don't know if she'll get it."

"Doesn't she have a position? Why is she here?" Berneen was trying to understand but felt too tired to make a start on that.

"Branigan told us that she quit her position and moved this way. Brady's happy, he said, that she did. I suspect he's more than a little interested in her." He turned her around. "Time to sleep, love. It's an early day for us in the morning."

"That it is." Berneen stopped. "I'll go see her later."

"Go on your own for now. The other ladies will want to meet her, but she's looking very overwhelmed right now."

Chapter 9

Later that morning, Fynn stood, the refrigerator door open, staring open mouthed into it. Someone had stocked it with fresh fruit and veggies, she thought. Her mind wandered to Brady. No, it hadn't been him. He hadn't been able to. Her face softened as she thought through what she knew of his friends and knew that one of the men or the ladies had done that. She hadn't had anyone treat her like that in years, she thought, other than Eric and his parents. Her own mother would have had to be asked to do that, and likely would have grumbled at doing it. Fynn frowned. Now, why would I think that? It's just so bizarre, how I am finding out what Mom and Dad would do and not do. Why? Lord, I could sure use some help here about now. I'm so confused. I hurt in more ways than one.

Hearing a tap at the door, Fynn moved that way, standing with her hand on the open door, watching the lady about her age who stood there, holding up a basket of muffins.

"I'm not sure if you've had breakfast, but I wanted to bring you these." Berneen tilted her head to study the other woman. Baird, you are so right. She is hurting in many ways. "I'm Berneen, Baird's wife."

"Berneen! Of course. Come on in. I'm sorry. Everything is such a struggle this morning." Fynn walked back into the kitchen. "Coffee? Or tea?"

"Water's fine." Berneen set the basket down and then surprised Fynn by reaching to hug her. "You've been through a lot, thrown into a building overrun with caring overprotective men and you're lost"

Fynn started laughing. "I don't know how you managed to sum it up so perfectly, but yes, that's about it."

Berneen grinned. "This is mild to what I have seen and what I went through." She pointed to the chair. "Can we sit? I need to tell you our story."

Fynn finally sat back, her eyes huge. "You did not go through all that?" She stared at her new friend as Berneen nodded.

"We did. I was held captive, Baird was taken captive. We were freed, kidnapped again and Buckley was forced to marry us to save Baird's life."

Fynn stared at her. "That doesn't happen in real life."

Berneen grinned at her. "For us, it did. Just like for Benen and Cadee. They married so she could get out of a South American country alive. Blair and Devaney were engaged years ago but she left him to try and save his life. Bradon and Ennis. Theirs is quite the story. Both almost died at the same time."

Fynn shook her head. "Brady didn't warn me. He should have." She jumped as she felt an arm come around her shoulder and turned her head.

Brady just grinned at her before he moved to fill a mug with coffee, returning to sit beside her. She stared at him and then past him at the two men filling their own mugs. Baird she recognized, sort of, from the night before. The other one, she shook her head. No, she didn't know him but she felt she should.

"How are you this morning?" Baird merely grinned at her as he sat beside his wife. "That good, huh?"

She shook her head at his half-smile. "I have no idea how I am to feel. I have never been in an accident before. Certainly not one where the driver couldn't control his vehicle."

The others laughed at the look on Brady's face and his protest.

"I didn't do it on purpose. Someone ran me off the road."

"That's your story. I didn't see another vehicle." She smirked at him as she said it.

His eyes narrowed as he caught the glint of mischief in her eyes. "How could you? You were sleeping."

"And I notice that you didn't wake me up to verify your story." She jumped as her phone chimed. She knew it was Eric and just let it go to voice mail.

The eyes of the other three kept bobbing between the two before Barnabas spoke.

"Do you remember what happened, Brady?"

Brady shrugged. "I can sort of remember a vehicle in my lane and trying to avoid it. I couldn't. It was done deliberately. I couldn't avoid him. I tried."

"We know you did, Brady." Barnabas watched him closely, Doc having spoken to him. "Dr. Daley, I am Barnabas Carey. We were to talk, but not like this."

She studied him for a moment before she spoke. "Please, it's Fynn. I think I left the doctor part behind. At least for now, I have. And we were?"

Barnabas smiled at her. "We were. Brady asked me to. I was going to let you get settled in, but it seems as if that isn't to be the case."

Fynn shook her head. "I have no idea what the case was to be." She groaned. "I thought I left all that behind me. I guess I haven't."

"Fynn, Brady said you were threatened."

Fynn slowly nodded. "I guess you could say I was. The thing is I have no idea who or why. I know others older than me were upset that I received the employment offer I did at my age. It is usually someone well experienced and older that gets them."

"We understand. So it could be someone from your work, someone who lost out of a position, or someone from your past." Barnabas had pulled out his pen, holding it posed above his notepad as he listened to her.

She sighed. "I suspect all three. If there are three after me, why go after Brady?"

"Will Peters, our police chief, has a detective looking into that as well. The detective will be out tomorrow to talk to you. No, wait, tomorrow's Sunday. He'll be out on Monday."

Fynn nodded, a question on her face as she turned to Brady, to find him watching her intently.

He gave a gentle smile. "We haven't introduced you yet. This is Barnabas Carey. He's the one you were going to speak to."

Her eyes shot back to Barnabas, before a frown settled on her face. "I'm not sure this is such a good idea after all."

"What isn't?" Barnabas had a good idea of what she was thinking, but waited for her to verbalized her thoughts.

"Moving here. Brady could have been killed yesterday, Did whoever it is follow me?"

"Or was I the one whoever it is was after?" Brady shook his head at her look. "That's a possibility. I have made enemies over the years without knowing it. I have been warned by the police about that."

"But it doesn't make sense that they would wait until now."

Chapter 10

Barnabas watched Brady closely, knowing he would be thinking the same thing.

"Who is after you then, Dr. Daley? Who wants to hurt you that bad?"

Fynn's eyes had flown to him as he spoke and then she sighed, her head dropping.

"Please, call me Fynn. I want to leave the doctor bit behind for now, if I even can." She shifted in her chair, not seeing the concern on the others' faces. "I don't know. I know my office was searched. Security couldn't figure out how it was done. My home was tossed as they say. I know I have been followed at times." She sighed once more. "I know there was one student who was really jealous of me in high school. A senior. He resented the fact that I was in the same grade and three years younger than him."

"I see. If you have names, please let us know. Branigan will look into them before we hand them over to Will Peters, our police chief."

Baird spoke, his eyes on Berneen, who was closely watching the couple across from her. "Not just Branigan. We'll all research. We've done it before."

"You have? How?" Fynn's mind took off on the possibilities, and they all realized they had just lost her. Brady was watching her, a grin on his face before he looked up.

"You lost her, Baird. She'll be thinking through how you do that. She may come up with an answer before you do." He watched as she reached for her phone, to scroll through her messages, before her fingers were flying over the keys.

Fynn sat back, knowing that Eric would head her way. He was in town, that much she knew.

"My cousin, Eric, he's in town. He's heading this way." She looked up, an apology on her face. "I'm sorry. I shouldn't have asked him to come."

"Fynn, let me say this once and only once." Barnabas waited until he had her attention. "This is your home. Yes, it is the Foundation building, but it is home to us all first and foremost. If your cousin is here, he is welcome to stay."

Brady spoke, knowing Fynn wouldn't say what she was thinking. "Eric is a police officer. He has just taken the empty detective spot on the force in Ennis' town."

She nodded. "I didn't know that he was moving, not until I said I was leaving town." She looked around at the four with her. "He's my cousin, but he's more like a big brother to me. I am an only child." Her voice died away. "No, I'm not an only child. God, please, don't let it be true." Her head went down on her folded arms.

Brady shot the others a look before his arm enveloped her and his head rested next to hers as she sobbed.

Berneen was on her feet, coming around to sit beside Fynn, her arms around her as Brady stood and moved away, anger showing on his face. Baird and Barnabas moved with him.

"Brady?"

"What?" Brady spun, the anger that had flared subsiding. "Sorry. I hate to see her like this. She doesn't open up to anyone, not this way."

"She's past her limit, Brady." Baird turned to watch the two ladies. "Coming here. The accident. Finding people who cared about her without knowing her." He looked back at Brady. "What did she mean?

"Mean what?" Brady shifted so he could see Fynn's face as she raised it, tears covering it, his heart breaking for her.

"When she said she wasn't an only child?"

Brady shrugged. "I have no idea."

"I'm not. I had an older brother, who just disappeared when I was about two. I had forgotten him. He was about four years older than me. No one ever talks about him." Fynn stood beside Brady. "Why?"

"They never talked to you, Fynn?"

Fynn spun as she heard Eric's voice. "Eric? What do you know?"

He shrugged. "No one seems to talk much about it but I did some research over the last few years. Your brother just seems to have disappeared when he was six. They could never find him. It's still an open case."

"That's so weird. Why would all his pictures disappear?"

"They have? I didn't know that. I know Mom has some. I'll get her to email me a couple and then we can look into it." He looked up at Brady, catching his look, and nodding, before he was introduced to the others.

"Brady? Have a moment?" Eric's voice was low, his eyes on Fynn.

'Sure. What's up?"

"I don't like that Fynn was never told. I don't know why she just remembered, but it could be dangerous for her. Mom said her parents received death threats against them and against Fynn. Fynn is smart. She's thrown herself into her studies and then her work, trying to please her parents."

"But she never could because she wasn't her brother." Brady's eyes slid closed as he sighed. "That's why they seem so distant to her, isn't it?"

"I would suspect so. I can't do much right now, but we can't let this lie. If her brother is still alive, where is he? And is he the one behind all this?"

"That's my fear, now that I know. How do we keep her safe? She's going to want to wander out in the forests and the fields, researching her creepy-crawlies." Brady grinned at the frown directed his way as Fynn moved into his space.

Chapter 11

Her mind not on where she was stepping, Fynn tripped over a small fallen branch in her way, just catching herself from hitting the ground. It had been four days since Eric had appeared, confirming that she was not an only child. He had passed on some photos from his mother but she didn't recognize her brother. Flannery, they said his name was. She didn't remember. Fynn had been just too young at the time.

She sighed, knowing that Brady would be looking for her. He had gone back to work the day before, insisting he was able to, but she had her doubts. She had seen the fatigue and pain in his face the night before and insisted that he just go to bed, not spending the time with her that he had planned. Brady had hesitated, wanting to be with her, before he sighed, nodded, gave her a tight hug and walked away.

Fynn stooped, her eyes on the creepy-crawlies Brady teased her about, not hearing the footsteps stealthily approaching from behind her. A scream that rose in her throat was cut off by the hand wrapped around her face even as an arm wrapped around her waist, trapping her own to her sides. She struggled, trying desperately to escape, her feet kicking at the legs of the man who held her. Fynn didn't hear the muttered words between the two men before she was carried at a rapid pace from the area and then through the shallow water to a waiting cabin cruiser. She was shoved roughly down the stairs and into a cabin, the door swung shut behind her and locked before she could regain her feet.

Propelled across the room, her legs struck the edge of the bunk and she fell forward, her arms out to stop herself. She spun and was on her feet, her hand on the door handle, twisting and yanking at it before she pounded at the door, calling for the men to let her go, to free her, that they must have the wrong person. Hearing no response, she stood, hand on the door handle, the other hand flat on the door itself as she twisted to study the room.

No, Fynn thought, there is no escape from here. I can't get out of the windows or whatever they are called on a boat. The locked door had trapped her. She finally slumped onto the bunk, her eyes studying the room, a calmness settling over her. Who were the men, she wondered, and why me?

She shuddered from sudden fear, a fear she had never known before. She willed the tears welling in her eyes back down before she blinked rapidly, rising to her feet to systematically search the cabin and attached bathroom, finding nothing that she could use for a weapon. Fynn paused for a moment, her eyes on the spray bottle of cleaning solution. If necessary, she would use that to protect herself.

Lord, why? Couldn't You have gotten my attention in some other way? For now, it's just You and me. I guess this is when I need to trust, isn't it? Lord, I need to heal. I have been hurting and struggling for so long, I don't know when I felt free. Help me to trust You, to lean on You. I have no idea what I am facing but You do.

Hours passed before she heard the door unlock and open. Fynn had refused to put on a light, sitting in the dimness of the dying day, her mind focusing on the verses that she could remember on trusting in danger, of peace, of God's protection in all things. She looked up through her lashes to see a tray set on the table near the door before the man, or youth, she thought, watched her as he backed away, the door shut and locked behind him. Fynn finally rose and walked over to study the tray, turning away, knowing that anything on it could harm her. The sandwich and fruit looked harmless, but she was taking no chances.

Fynn searched for a pen and paper, finding some stuck away deep in a drawer and sat back on the bunk, switching on a light overhead. She tapped the pen idly against her mouth before she back to jot notes and then scribble furiously as her thoughts flew. Who was it, she wondered? Someone she knew? Someone she didn't know but who knew her? Someone from one of the cases she had worked on?

She settled back against the pillows, her legs drawn up as she curled up on her side and finally slept. Her last thought was for Brady, praying for his healing from their accident and for protection. She had no idea if her captors would go after him, but she suspected that they would, if she couldn't or wouldn't tell them what they wanted. And just what that was she had no idea. Maybe tomorrow they would tell her. She slept, not feeling the gentle swaying of the boat as the waves rocked it in the night.

Mid-morning, she turned from where she had been watching the water, trying to determine if the boat was still in the same spot. She thought it was, but wasn't quite sure. She watched as a man entered, an older man, stooped, his hair unkempt, a straggly beard on his face. He paced towards her and then back towards the door, his hands to his sides, clenched into fists.

"Where is he?" When Fynn didn't respond, he stalked towards her, stopping just short of touching her. "I said, where is he?"

"Where's who?" Fynn's head tilted to the side, her eyes looking past the man at the youth standing just outside the door. He's the one from last night, she thought. Who is he?

"You know who I mean. Where is he?"

Fynn shrugged. "I have no idea who you mean. And just where am I? I would like to go home, if you don't mind."

"Not yet. Not until you tell me where he is." The man lumbered away, an unkempt smell lingering in the air after him that roiled Fynn's stomach, and that took a lot to do, given the situations she found herself in. She watched as the door was closed and heard the lock sound before she sighed and then sat carefully on the edge of the bunk.

She had discovered that there were loose boards on the bunk, and she had hidden one under the thin mattress with the hopes that she just might be able to use it to escape. Fynn's thoughts turned to Brady, wishing she could see him, needing to feel his strength of character to help her through what she was facing.

She sighed to herself, not knowing who the man was that she had been asked about. Her brow furrowed as a thought passed through her mind before she shook her head. It couldn't be her brother, the one she had forgotten about. That would be just too strange.

Chapter 12

Fatigue weighing his body down, Brady slid from his truck seat and shut the door, leaning back on it to close his eyes. He hurt worse today than he did yesterday, if that was possible. He shook his head, regretting it as the headache that had lingered behind his eyes all day came out in full force. He shifted the duffle bag he carried to his other hand and reached for his keys as he headed for the building and his apartment. He didn't see Breck watching him closely before he followed him, concern on his face at the slowness of Brady's walk.

Brady eyed the stairs to the second floor and then headed for an elevator, not up to the climb that night. He paused as he exited the elevator, his eyes tracing down the hall to the apartment Fynn had been assigned, but shook his head once more. He needed to clean up before he sought her company.

His heavy work boots hit the tray in the hall closet before he detoured through the kitchen to flick on the coffeemaker he had left ready to start that morning. He dropped his duffle bag in the laundry room before heading for a shower.

Refreshed to some degree, he gathered his dirty clothes and headed back for the laundry, dropping them and the contents of his bag into the washer and setting it. He reached for the coffee carafe to pour a cup of coffee before he opened the fridge door, staring in and then closing it. He wasn't ready to eat, not just yet.

Brady headed for the door of Fynn's apartment, puzzled when she didn't answer. He shrugged, figuring she was outside somewhere and headed that way himself, searching through the seating areas before standing at the building entrance, a hand on his head, his eyes narrowing as she searched. He jumped as he felt a hand come down on his shoulder.

"Brady? How are you feeling today?" Blair stood there, the other men gathering around them.

"Sore." He searched the faces to his friends, his heart sinking at the grim looks on their faces. "Guys? What's up?" When no one answered, he turned to Blair. "Blair? What's going on? I don't like the looks on your faces."

"And we don't like what we have to tell you. Fynn has disappeared. Bradon and Kade tracked her for a while until Kade lost her scent."

"Disappeared? How? When?"

"We think sometime early this afternoon. Berneen had met her for lunch and then Fynn told her she wanted to be outdoors, to look for her creepy-crawlies as you call them."

"I thought so." Brady's shoulders slumped. "I tried to reach her around two and didn't get an answer. But then she tends to leave her phone on mute." He looked around at his friends, seeing Barnabas walking his way accompanied by Will. "You've reported it?"

"We have. Given her profession and the threats from her hometown, Will has made it a matter of importance right now. There are officers out there searching. We need to go through her apartment." Blair looked around. "What about her cousin?"

"I spoke with him this morning. He's had to go back north to finalize his move here. He's on the road somewhere, I think. I'll call him in a bit." Brady straightened, his eyes on Will. "Will? Any word?"

Will studied his young friend, his heart hurting for him. "Nothing yet. Our own K-9 teams have tracked where they could, same as Bradon and Kade. They lose her scent."

"And that means she wasn't walking then, doesn't it?" Brady paced away from them, not willing to let them see how upset he was, not knowing that they knew. His four friends who had already faced something like this exchanged glances. Brady paced back towards Barnabas. "Has anyone checked her apartment?"

Barnabas nodded. "Breck did earlier. Anna went with him. Fynn's phone was on the kitchen table. There were no signs that she had been back and then left again."

"So, where is she?" Brady walked away, pausing to turn. "Where was she?"

"Near the lake, and you can't go that way yet, Brady." Will's words stopped Brady as he turned. "There's a crime scene there we are processing." He shook his head at the look on Brady's face. "It is a crime scene, Brady. You know that."

"I know." Brady walked past his friends, to slump down onto one of the couches in the foyer, Branigan sitting beside him, just waiting.

Buckley watched from the chair he had chosen to sit in for a few moments before he began to pray. Brady's heart quieted as he listened.

He's right, Lord, Brady prayed. You are in control of this. You do have Fynn in the hollow of Your hand. I just want her here with me. Yes, she is becoming that important to me. I never believed in love at first sight, but that's what happened. Is she the one You've chosen for me? Please, dear Lord, bring her home.

His mind drifting, Brady tuned out the quiet conversation between the two men, concentrating on the verses of protection and healing that he could think of. He knew Fynn needed to heal, in just so many ways. He hurt that she was gone, that he didn't know where she was.

Finally, Brady stood, a thought crossing his mind and he walked towards the stairs, leaving his friends staring after him before they exchanged glances and then shrugged. He shut his apartment door quietly, standing for a moment leaning against it, his head back and his eyes closed. He knew God was in control, that He was leading him with that thought. He reached for his phone as he walked towards his office, sliding down into the leather chair with a sigh. He hurt too much to sit but he had to. He needed to research.

"Eric?" Brady could hear the quiet conversation that surrounded Eric coming faintly through the phone.

"Brady? Why are you calling me? Hold on a sec."

Brady heard Eric asking for his bill and then his quiet thanks as he paid it.

"Okay, I'm in my vehicle. What's up?"

"Fynn."

"Fynn? Isn't she with you? That's what she said this morning, that she would be spending the evening with you. Her words were along the line that Brady would occupy her evening with a walk and quiet conversation." Eric waited, not hearing Brady reply. "Brady? Where is Fynn?"

"That we don't know, Eric. She's disappeared. Sometime this afternoon. We're looking for her but haven't found her. It's like she disappeared into thin air." Brady waited, hearing the silence on the other end of the phone

"I'm on my way back."

"No, finish what you need to. If anything, Barnabas will send Andy up with the plane and have one of our security guards come to so he can drive your vehicle back."

Eric was torn, wanting to be in on the search for Fynn but knowing he had to be in his hometown on the next day. "Okay, I'll finish what I need to quickly and head back down. I should be able to be on the road before noon. Call me, please?"

"I will. Pray, Eric. Just pray for her to come home." Brady set his phone down, staring at it, before he pulled up a search engine on his computer and starting searching, hunting for what he didn't know. He didn't hear Branigan and Baird enter, followed by Benen.

"Brady? What are you up to?"

Benen's voice caused Brady to spin, surprise on his face. "I'm trying to research her brother. Does that make sense?"

"It does. It seems to come back to him." Benen motioned him. "Let me. I might have more resources that you do."

Brady stood, his hand extended to his chair. "Be my guest." He began to pace, stopping in surprise as a mug appeared in front of his face. He took it with a quiet thanks to Baird, before he found a chair and slumped down into it, pain evident on his face. He needed to take something but couldn't, he thought. He started to shake his head as the medication bottle appeared in front of him and then nodded, reaching for it and shaking out two pills before he swallowed them, his eyes going back to Benen. Please, Lord, let us solve this. Let my lady come back home.

Chapter 13

Every day, Brady walked the woods surrounding the building, searching. Searching for anything that would help them find Fynn. Sometimes one of his friends was with him, quite often Bradon with his dog, Kade. He didn't want to show it, but he was becoming discouraged and downhearted that he would find her. His heart weighed heavy. He knew his friends and Dallas, the detective assigned to the case, were searching, trying to come up with a culprit or a suspect, and Benen and Eric, he knew, were searching for any word on her brother. No one had said anything to Brady, and he found that odd.

Brady sighed. He looked up, searching the sky for answers, seeing the heavy rain clouds moving in. He prayed for her return, but so far, God had not answered, or maybe He had and Brady had missed it. He turned for home, not finding peace that day, feeling agitated more and more. He was unable to really eat, but Anna had insisted that he take his meals with Doc and herself, mothering her as she did them all. Barnabas had been quiet, not saying much, but he kept a watch on Brady.

His phone ringing startled him and he paused, staring at the number for a moment before he answered. A quick conversation and he was off on a run. He was needed at work, to replace a coworker who had been injured. He couldn't say no, now could he?

Breck watched as he pulled away, a hand rubbing at his face. He had wanted to talk to Brady, to bring him up to date on their investigations. He would have to wait, he thought, before turning as he heard his name called.

"Breck? Have you seen Brady?" Burnie walked towards him at a rapid pace. "I just got off the phone with someone, and I need to talk to him."

Breck nodded towards the road. "He's off. I suspect he's heading in to work. I heard one of the paramedics was hurt today."

"Oh, no. That's not good." Burnie turned in a circle. "I can feel someone watching us."

"There is. Security has mentioned that they have found traces of that, but no one is around when they find those traces. We've passed it on to Dallas, and he had a crime scene team come up and look around. They haven't said much about what they found."

"I don't think they will. Listen, Blair and I are heading down to the lake to search. We've seen the same cabin cruiser anchored off shore for the last few days."

Breck spun, his eyes on Burnie. "For how long?"

Burnie paused, his face paling before growing stern. "For as long as Fynn has been missing. You don't think?"

"I do think. Come on. I'm with you. Let's see what we can find. I would love to be able to give Brady good news tonight. It's going to be a hard enough day for him as it is."

"That it will." Burnie paced towards where Blair waited and took the backpack he was offered. "Breck's with us."

"Sure. I thought he would be." Blair grinned as he handed over a pack to Breck. "Here you go. Devaney gave me three, although at the time I questioned why. Now, I know. She would just tell me God told her to."

"And she would be right." Breck followed after Burnie. "Before we go too far, let's pray. I just have a feeling about today."

"You and me both." Burnie paused and turned, nodding at Blair to pray.

Blair's prayer lifted Fynn up to God, pleading that she would come home and that they would find her that day. He lifted his head as his eyes opened, a confidence in his look that said God would answer their prayers that very day.

The three men searched together, then moved a ways apart, their eyes watchful, looking for any sign of Fynn or her abductors. Burnie paused for a moment, a water bottle raised to his lips, before he lowered it and capped it, a frown on his face before he was running forward, startling the two men with him, who followed, puzzled glances exchanged between them.

Burnie paused, his head tilted as he listened, his hand raised to still the question on Blair's lips, before he was off again. The other two men followed, seeing him drop to his knees in the longer grass, before they heard quiet murmurs coming from him. They ran after him, fighting their way through the grass that attempted to entangle itself around their legs and ankles and trip them. They paused, wonder on their face, before praises were raised.

Burnie had dropped to his knees, his eyes on Fynn, watching as she lay in a huddled heap, her head burrowed under an arm. His hand was tentative as he reached for her, feeling for a pulse and then he sat back on his heels.

"Burnie?" Breck's quiet question had Burnie raising his head and looking up, nodding. Breck's eyes slid closed in an inaudible prayer.

"She's alive, but bad she's hurt, I don't know." He reached for her again, finding her shifting away from him and sitting up, fear on her face as she stared at him before looking up at the other two.

Fynn's gaze stopped on Blair, and she studied him, her mouth opening and closing before she spoke in a hoarse whisper.

"I know you. Don't I know you?" She shifted backwards as Blair crouched in front of her.

"You do, Fynn. I'm a friend."

"You are? What's your name?"

"I'm Blair. I'm a friend of Brady's."

"Brady? Who's he?" She studied Blair before looking at the other two men, confusion in her gaze.

"He's a friend of yours." Blair extended his hand. "Can you stand and walk? We can take you to him."

She shook her head. "I can't. I can't go near him."

""Why not?" Breck's question had her head spinning his way, her hand to it as her eyes slid closed and she crumpled once more to the ground.

Blair watched for a moment before he stood and gathered her into his arms, her arms around his neck in an unconscious movement. "Hold on, Fynn. I'll carry you. You don't seem too steady on your feet." He looked around at Burnie's indrawn breath.

"She can't walk, Blair. Not on those feet." Burnie gently raised one, his hand grasping her ankle as she tried to pull back. "She has no shoes, but it looks as if she's done some walking, and that over some rough ground."

Breck nodded. "If she came up from the lake, and I suspect she did, it's really rough with shoes on. I don't know how she made it this far." He turned. "Let's get her to the infirmary. Doc was home when we left. He said he had planned to catch up on some reading. Anna and Amy are away from the day. Barnabas had told Amy to take the day off."

Reaching the building, Blair headed for the corridor that led to the infirmary, the security guard running ahead to unlock it. Burnie headed to find Doc, Breck following Blair. He watched as Blair gently laid Fynn on the bed and then moved back to stand beside him.

"Did she say anything at all?" Breck's question was low.

"Not a word. Nothing since those few sentences." His phone was out. "I need to let Dallas and Will know." He paused. "We need to call Eric. What time will Brady be out?"

"I don't know but it was only a part shift he picked up." Breck eyed his watch. "Likely soon. We'll need to watch for him." His head turned as he heard rapid footsteps coming his way. "Here's Doc."

"It's Fynn?" Doc's voice was hopeful.

"It is, Doc. She was awake for a bit before she passed out again. We found her about a mile from the lake."

"The lake? The boat that's been there?"

Breck nodded. "That's what we think. Which one of the ladies do you want?"

"Cadee, I think. She's helped in the clinic at the mission. Though Berneen seems to have made contact with Fynn that the others haven't."

"I'll go find Cadee then. Berneen, Devaney and Ennis were away this afternoon. Cadee wasn't able to go." Blair turned, to find Cadee standing beside him. "Cadee? How did you know?"

"Burnie. He came and found me. He's rounding up the others, he said, and they'll watch for Brady."

"Good. Call us if you need us, Doc." Blair stepped back from the room, his hand pulling the door closed behind him, his eyes seeing the others waiting. "Don't ask how she is, guys. I really don't know at this point."

Chapter 14

His eyes on Fynn, Doc hesitated a moment to pray, as he always did before he assessed a patient, before he moved towards her. Cadee stood on the other side of the bed, her hand on Fynn's, staring in disbelief.

"How, Doc?"

Doc shrugged. "I don't know, other than God. The three of them went searching and Burnie found her. She was out of it, his words, when they found her, roused for a few minutes, and then passed out again." Even as he spoke, Doc was at work, in physician mode now, assessing her. "Cadee, Burnie said her feet were hurt."

Cadee moved to look. "Oh, my, Doc. They are. She has no shoes on, did you know that?"

Doc shook his head. "No, I didn't. I'll take a look in a moment. We'll need the saline to rinse them off." He looked up. "Are you up for that?"

Cadee snorted, bringing a grin to Doc's face. "You should have seen what I had to help with. This is nothing. But I've never had to work on a close friend before."

"Is that what she is, Cadee? A close friend?"

"I know it's only a few days, but I would like to think that, Doc. She needs us." Cadee blinked back tears as she spoke, before she turned, hunting for the saline solution and then the cloths, bandages and basin that Doc needed, without being told what to find.

Doc watched her for a moment, before he nodded. He would need to talk to Benen, but Cadee was a natural nurse. If she had training, then he could use her here and perhaps at the mission where he volunteered. He knew she was looking for something, had been for a while now, not quite sure what she wanted to do.

"Doc?" He looked up at Cadee's quiet question. "Does Brady know?"

"I'm not sure. He had been called in to relieve someone this afternoon." His head turned as he heard scuffling in the hallway and the sound of a louder voice than had been heard. "I would say Brady's out there right now, and not happy he can't come in."

"That's what I wondered. Fynn hasn't said anything but I see how she watches him, without him knowing. She's in love with him, Doc."

"That may be, Cadee, but it's a discussion those two need to have. All we can do is pray for them."

Cadee sighed, knowing Doc was right, but wanting Brady and, yes, Fynn, to find the happiness she and Benen had found.

Doc worked away, his mouth in a tight, grim line as he treated Fynn's feet, finding wrapping them and then stepping back, a hand wiping at his face. He headed for the cabinets to pull out a bag of intravenous solution and the tubing and needle before he paused, then nodded. God, You did protect her. Thank you. He returned to Fynn's side to start the IV drip before he once more stood to watch her.

"Brady will want to come in, you know." Cadee grinned at Doc.

"I know he will. But first, I want to keep her here tonight. Can you stay for a bit? Anna will be back soon and she'll be here all night."

"I can. Doc, her feet?"

"I know, Cadee. She'll not be walking for a bit, that's a given. How she managed to get to where they found her, I'll never know. She's cut the one quite severely. Bruises, scrapes and minor nicks on both."

"But how, Doc? Wasn't she wearing shoes?"

Doc shook his head at Cadee's question. "No. She didn't have any on when I got here and Burnie said she wasn't wearing any."

"So, what happened to them? It's not like Fynn to wander around outside in her bare feet, at least, not out there." Cadee was puzzled, as she stared at her friend.

"No, it's not. That's something Will and Dallas will have to discover." Doc reached for his stethoscope once more before he stepped back again.

"Doc?"

"Hmm?" He looked around at Cadee before he smiled. "She's in good shape overall. Now, let's see about getting Brady in here."

Chapter 15

His feet dragging as he walked towards the back entrance of the building, Brady paused before he entered, his eyes drifting towards the lake. I'll search there tonight, Lord. I might even make my way out to that cabin cruiser and see what is up with it. It's been anchored there for so long, it makes me think it has something to do with Fynn's disappearance. Closing his apartment door behind him, his boots hit the tray in closet and he headed for the kitchen. It had been a stressful day, and he had already been worn out before he had headed into work.

He reached for clean jeans and a favourite T-shirt after his shower and shave before going back to the kitchen, reaching for his coffee and then for the sandwich he had made earlier but hadn't eaten. He had just taken a sip of coffee and bit into the sandwich when a knock came at his door. Brady stood, sandwich in one hand, his other hand of the door as he studied Blair standing there, puzzled at the look on his friend's face.

"Brady? You just get in? We were watching for you." Blair stepped inside as Brady moved back towards the kitchen.

"I came in the back way. Just wanted to grab a bite to eat before I head for the lake." Brady spun to face Blair. "I want to check out that cabin cruiser. It's been hanging around there for too long."

"Brady, before you go out, we need to talk." Blair sighed in frustration as Brady ignored him to finish his sandwich, take a last swig of his coffee, clicking off the coffeemaker and then reaching for a water bottle from the fridge. "Brady? Can you stop for a moment?"

Brady turned, surprised at the frustration evident in Blair's tone. "I can, but I do want to head that way. What's your problem?" He headed away from Blair, intent on finding his sneakers and shoving his feet into them.

"We found her, Brady." Blair waited, finally shaking his head, and stalking over to stand in front of the door, stopping Brady in his tracks.

Brady stood, a frown on his face. "Blair? What is it?"

"Fynn. We found her. She's here in the infirmary." Blair watched as Brady turned away from him. He saw the exact moment he understood his words.

Brady spun back, surprise and then hope on his face. "What did you say?"

"Fynn. Burnie, Breck and I found her. She's downstairs." Blair's hand came out to stop Brady's forward motion. "Doc and Cadee are with her. Dallas and Will are on their way out. They will need to talk to her first. If she's awake, that is."

"She's alive?" Brady didn't dare breathe, waiting for Blair to answer. "Blair? Please? How is she?"

"She's hurt, but I am not sure how bad. I haven't talked to Doc yet. She was unconscious when Burnie found her, talked for a bit, and then slipped away again. Her feet are torn up. Doc can tell you more." Blair's hand on Brady's chest kept him from moving forward and through the door, he was that anxious to find his lady. "Before you go, let's pray, Brady. She didn't remember who we were."

Brady nodded. "Given what she's been through, she'll have shut down to some extent. She'll remember us."

Blair snorted. "Remember you, you mean. Don't deny it, Brady. She's your lady."

Brady reached to brush away Blair's hand, not answering his unspoken question, before he was out of the door and heading for the stairs at a rapid pace. Blair swung the door closed behind him and was on Brady's heels, a hand out again to stop him.

"Brady, wait. We need to pray. We didn't."

Brady stopped, his head dropping forward, his eyes closing. He had forgotten. He had been in such a rush to get to Fynn, he had forgotten Blair had asked to pray.

"I'm sorry, Blair. You're right. Please?"

Blair nodded, his prayer quiet, raising Fynn up to God for healing, for Brady as he struggled to work, for the couple who were such new friends but had made a connection. He prayed for swift resolution of the mystery surrounding Fynn's disappearance, for protection for the two, and for wisdom for the police services as they sought to understand and then arrest the ones involved.

Brady raised his head, a thought crossing his mind. "Does Eric know?"

"I'm not sure. Will was reaching out to the chief in Ennis' town."

The two walked down the stairs, Brady's thoughts muddled as he approached the infirmary, heading for the door before he was stopped. He glared at Baird standing in his way, before he tried to shove by him. Hands reached to stop him and pull him backwards. Brady hit the wall and then tried to escape the hands holding him there. This was the scuffle Doc had heard and smiled at.

Will smiled and shook his head before nodding to Dallas to proceed to the infirmary. Will stood in front of Brady, his eyes searching the younger man, before he nodded. Will's wife had been correct in her assessment. Brady cared deeply for Fynn, he could see. The devastation and stress had taken a toll on Brady, he could see it in his face and in the lost weight. Brady had never been heavy, Will knew that, but the few pounds he had lost over the last week showed. Fynn's disappearance and the pain from his accident were all part of that, Will knew from experience.

Dallas tapped at the door before cracking it open and peeking around it, seeing Doc motioning him to enter.

"Doc? Talk to me. How is she?"

Doc shook his head. "To tell you the truth, other than her feet, she's in good shape."

"Her feet?" Dallas frowned, a pen and notepad in hand, as he waited.

"Her feet. They're torn up, but that would be from her walk up through the rocks and then the woods. She was on her way here, but I'm not sure she remembers that. She didn't have any shoes on her feet by the looks of it."

Dallas nodded. "Any other injuries?"

Doc nodded. "When we raised the head of the bed a bit ago, she was in pain. Her back is bruised, I would say from falling against something. It doesn't look like she has been abused or beaten. She's dehydrated, has lost weight. She doesn't give the appearance of having been drugged, but I drew blood and sent it in to the lab to verify that."

"Good." Dallas shot a look back at the door. "Now, is she awake that I can talk to?"

Doc shook his head, his eyes of Cadee as she pulled the sheet and light blanket up higher on Fynn's shoulders. "She's been drifting in and out, but she sleeping now. I have no idea how long she'll sleep for."

Dallas tucked away his pen and notepad. "About what I figured you'd say. I'll talk to the three who found her. Will sent a team out to where she was, but I don't think we'll find anything." He paused. "Interestingly, that cabin cruiser has disappeared."

"That's where she'll have been then, on it. So close yet so far away." Doc turned to Dallas. "Find out who did this before either one of them is hurt again."

Chapter 16

Looking up as his captain sat in a chair by his desk, Eric drew a deep breath. He had been burning the candle, he thought, at both ends, working the cases he had been assigned and trying to make good doing that, and then searching for Fynn and researching for any information he could find on Flannery.

"Eric? How is it going for you? Fitting in okay?" Captain Walters had taken the call from Will and was relieved for his new detective. It would mean one load of stress would be lifted from Eric's shoulders, but another added, as the detectives searched for Fynn's abductors.

"I am. The group is great, sharing tips and helping out. Not what I had expected, given the experience I had on my old force. There was always a reluctance to share information." Eric's gaze dropped to the report he had just finished and printed. He had closed the case of the armed robbery at a local convenience store, but still had cases that were open and needing his attention. He looked back up, catching a look on his Captain's face that he frowned at. "Captain?"

"Please, call me Jim. The others do. We're part of the same church family, as well." Jim paused, his eyes on the fingers he was rubbing together. "I received a call from Chief Peters a bit ago."

Eric straightened up in his chair, his eyes not moving from Jim's face. "And?"

"Three of Brady's friends went searching this afternoon." Jim shook his head. "It had to be God, that's all we can say."

"Fynn?" Eric's voice was barely above a whisper. He had talked to his mother that morning, who had called, concerned. He frowned as he remembered her words that Fynn's parents had left on a planned vacation three days earlier, without waiting to find out if Fynn was safe or not.

"She's safe. They found her." Jim watched with compassion as Eric tried to control his emotions. He knew from his conversations with Eric how important Fynn was to him, that he considered her the sister he never had.

"Thank God." Eric looked up. "And, how is she?"

"In good shape." Jim pointed at the desk. "Where are you with your work? At a point you can leave it?"

"I just finished the report on the armed robbery, but I was to interview the bank teller." Eric was torn, wanting to head for Fynn, but wanting to prove himself.

"Do your interview and then head out. I've put Leslie on call. He came and volunteered, hearing the rumours that Fynn was found."

"He did? He didn't have to." Eric was surprised but thankful. He enjoyed the crew of detectives he was paired with.

"No, he didn't, but that's what we do here, Eric. We share the burdens of all our people, not just our own. Head out when you're ready. Call me if you think you need tomorrow."

Eric's head was down as he prayed, not watching Jim walk away. He was so grateful that Fynn was alive and safe. He reached for the file that was waiting and rose, heading for the interview room and the bank teller.

His thoughts on Eric and wondering if he had been called, Brady's head went back against the wall. He had struggled with his friends to get to the door but had been held back. He finally nodded to them and their hands dropped away, even as concern for both he and Fynn coloured their faces. He couldn't pray, didn't know how to frame his words, but he knew God understood, that at this time was when the Holy Spirit prayed for him. He looked up to see Will in front of him.

"Brady?" Will's voice held a question he didn't ask, that he wanted to know how Brady really was.

"I'm okay, Will. The guys would say otherwise, but I am okay." He gave a quick grin at the comments and quiet laughter that reached his ears. "How is she?"

"I haven't talked to Doc. That's Dallas' job. I am here for you, my friend." Will's heart uttered a prayer as he saw Brady taking in his words before he nodded. "And yes, Eric will have been told. I talked to his Captain earlier. It depends on what Eric has on his desk that he has to deal with today before he can head over."

"Thanks, Will." Brady's gaze went past him as the door opened and Dallas approached him, stopping just short of where Will stood, a shuttered look on his face. Brady's heart sank.

"Go on in, Brady. She's sleeping right now. I'll talk with her later." Dallas shared a glance with Will, who nodded, knowing that Dallas would not leave that building until he had had that talk with her.

Brady shoved away from the wall, his legs feeling weak for a moment, before he walked towards the door, his hand resting on it for a moment before he shoved it open. He knew his friends would hang around for a while before they headed for their own places, or perhaps the chapel. He knew Buckley would stay around close, ready to be his pastor instead of just his friend. That he was grateful for. A sudden thought crossed his mind. How did people who had no faith manage situations like this? He knew he wouldn't have handled it as well if it had not been for his own faith and trust in God.

Dallas watched as the other men lingered for a while and then left before he turned to Will. Barnabas had not left, standing watching Dallas closely

"Will? What do we know of Brady's past? Could it be part of this?"

Will shrugged and turned to Barnabas. "Barnabas?"

"Brady is from Nova Scotia. I found him just as he graduated from high school and offered him a position here. It was his decision to become a paramedic. He said his father had been one and had died on the job, working a flood when Brady was around ten. His mother never got over it, he said, dying from what Brady termed as a broken heart when he was seventeen. He was in foster care until he graduated high school. I can have the guys look into it for you."

"I have been, Barnabas." Dallas frowned, then grimaced. "I hate going behind his back."

"He understands that you would have been looking into him as well. He mentioned that last night, in fact." Barnabas shook his head. "I just want this over for him and Fynn and something tells me it isn't."

"Not yet. Not until we find her abductors and solve that."

Chapter 17

Letting the door close quietly behind him, Brady stood, his eyes on Doc, who nodded at him to approach, then on Cadee, who gave him a gentle smile before she too pointed at the bed. His eyes dropped to Fynn, watching for a moment before he walked forward, hesitation in his steps. He stood, one hand clutching tightly to the bed rail, before he reached to touch her hair, one curl tucking between his fingers and wrapping around one. He waited for her to rouse but she lay still.

Brady studied her face, seeing the lines and shadows and hollows in it that were new. He sighed. Lord, why? Why Fynn? Who did she anger so much that this happened to her? I pray for healing for her.

He reached for her free hand, tucked near her cheek. She tightened her grip on his even as she sighed and shifted to her side, to face him, her grip tightening even more as he tried to free his own. Doc just shook his head, knowing these two were in love with one another, whether they had acknowledged it or not.

Brady prayed as he hadn't before. He needed Fynn to wake up. Yes, he acknowledged to himself that he needed her in his life. He prayed that she would be agreeable. The last week had been no difficult, not having her there. He had missed her, her dry sense of humour, her teasing, but also the deep thoughts she brought forth, thoughts she said she never shared with anyone else not even Eric. He did that to her, she accused, a smile on her face as she said it. Brady knew that she made him think, to delve back into the Bible to prove or disprove her thoughts.

Fynn stirred, a hand wiping at the hair on her forehead, brushing it back, even as her eyes opened. She stared at the navy T-shirt in her line of sight and frowned. Who was that? It was too tall for Eric, and her father wouldn't have been there, not in a hospital room, and that was where she was convinced she was. She gave a soft moan as she moved, the bruising on her back painful but the pain and soreness of her feet stronger than that.

"Fynn? Darlin'? You awake?" Brady's voice was low enough that only Fynn could hear him. He didn't realize he had slipped in an endearment, he was that focused on her opening eyes.

"Go away." Fynn's tone was disgruntled.

"Sorry, darlin'. No happening. Come on, love. Wake up." Brady's face held a small smile, but underneath it was the concern and worry he was trying so hard to hide.

"I'm sorry. Do I know you?" Fynn rolled slightly to look up, way up, she thought, at Brady, not realizing that he still held her hand. That was something she never allowed. No one held her hand, but Brady made her feel safe.

"You do. I'm Brady. We met a few weeks ago when I found a body and you were brought in. I've missed you the last week. We haven't been out to look for your creepy-crawlies." He grinned as she frowned at him.

"Creepy-crawlies? Really?" She gave a soft sigh. "I remember. You're the reason I moved, did you know that?" She frowned as he grinned at her. "It's not funny."

"No, it's not. How are you feeling?" He bent closer, a hand reaching to cup her cheek.

She gripped that hand, her mind working to remember. "I think I'm okay. But I don't know where I am, other than not on that boat."

"You're in the Foundation Building. Barnabas had set up an infirmary for it. That's where you are. And likely will be overnight, if I know Doc." Brady's head turned slightly as he heard Doc moving closer.

"Doc? Do I know him?" Fynn turned her head slightly, her eyes sliding closed at the sudden onset of a headache. "My head hurts."

"Of course it does. You're dehydrated. That would do it." Doc reached for her wrist, all the while watching her face. "I'll keep you here overnight. Anna will be alone shortly, but for now, Cadee is here. But now that you're awake, we need to get Dallas in here to talk to you." He paused, a smile on his face at her frown. "He's the detective who has your case, as they say."

"And before you ask, Eric will be here shortly. At least I think he will."

"Real definite there, buster." Fynn's eyes closed as she swallowed hard. "Did they find them?"

"Find who?" Dallas spoke from where he stood at the end of the bed.

"The men." Fynn frowned at him. "I don't know you, but I pray you're the detective I can tell my story too and then I need to sleep. I haven't slept in a week."

"Let me take your statement, and then I'll disappear. We'll find the men, Fynn. We will find them. We're searching. Brady's friends are searching. Your cousin and the men and women on that force are searching. The police chief from your hometown has been in touch, wanting to know what they can do to help." He held up a hand at her protest. "It's what we do for anyone, Fynn. But you're one of us, whether or not you are still doing your forensics stuff, as Baird calls it."

Fynn nodded, her eyes on him. "I guess that means Brady and Doc and Cadee have to leave."

"Doc stays. Brady and Cadee need to step outside for now. I want Doc here to monitor you and to tell you to stop if you. need to." Dallas nodded as Brady took a reluctant step away, his eyes on Fynn's face before he walked to the door, holding it open for Cadee, and then stepping through himself, the door closing almost on his heels.

Chapter 18

His pen poised over his notepad, his computer set to record her voice, Dallas waited, watching as Doc spoke quietly to her and then handed her a glass of water to drink. Fynn's hand shook as she took it, Doc's hand reaching to help her bring the glass to her mouth and drink. She nodded when she was finished, her eyes on her now-clasped hands.

"Where do I start, Dallas, is it?" Her voice was low, taut, shaky as she strove to control her emotions.

"Talk to me about that day. What did you do, what you had planned." He nodded at her look. "It's okay. It can be part of the statement." He watched as she swallowed and sighed to himself. It's never easy when you're the professional who has to be on the other side of the coin.

Fynn looked up at him, knowing that they were things she would never tell him. She suspected he knew that. "Okay. I guess I can. This is not easy. I never knew how the victims would feel. I never talk to the families. I stay in the background."

Fynn reached for the glass, sipping slowly as she thought through what she needed to say. She shuddered at the remembered feel on the man's hand around her mouth.

"I had had lunch with the ladies here and then went out. I was just walking, taking a look around, getting to know the area. I wanted to start a study on the bugs and insects indigient to the area, just in case I do go back to my work. I had headed towards the lake. As I remember it, I was bent over or crouching down when I felt a hand come around my face, over my mouth, and another arm wrapping around me, trapping my arms to my sides. I fought. How I fought to get free, but I couldn't. I was carried away towards the lake. I thought I was going to be drowned but instead I was dumped into a small rowboat. I tried to jump out, but the man grabbed my arm and held a knife out towards me. He forced me up a ladder, across the deck and then down some stairs before he shoved me hard enough into a cabin that I landed on a bunk. I tried to get out but the door was locked.

"I didn't sleep well, couldn't in fact. I searched for a way out but there was none. Twice a day a youth, an older teenager I think, would bring in a tray and take away the one he had left. I refused to eat." Fynn paused to catch her breath. "I had water from the small washroom, I wouldn't touch what was on the tray."

She blinked rapidly, her eyes unfocused for a moment as a puzzled look crossed her face. "Every morning and then again in the afternoon, the man who threatened me appeared. He didn't stay for long, just kept asking where someone was. Where is he, was what he asked. He didn't give a name at all. Never in all the times he questioned me. I found that odd. I had to say I didn't know. I didn't. It was just so bizarre."

She looked up at Dallas, finding him watching her intently. "That last morning, the youth left the tray. I was by the window, port, porthole, whatever it is called, not looking back at him. I had tried to make my way out of it, but it was too small. When he left, I waited for the door to lock. I still don't know if he left it open on purpose or just forgot. I waited for about an hour and then approached it, not sure what I would find. The door was, as I suspected, unlocked. I went out, watching for the men, but didn't see them. Not even on the deck. The cruiser was deserted. I climbed down the ladder and then had to swim for shore. I was so afraid. I had heard of tides in the area that took unsuspecting swimmers away from the shore

"Once on shore, I walked towards the rocks, forgetting I had no shoes. The man who questioned me took them from me on the second day. I fought him to keep them. That's when he shoved me back against the corner of the wall, and I hit it hard with my back. I couldn't stop him from leaving."

Fynn blinked rapidly once more, her thoughts on the trek she had made. "I walked as fast as I could, stumbling over debris, my feet hitting rocks and stones. I think that's when I cut my foot. I remember a sharp pain and dropping down, wrapping my hand on my foot and seeing blood. I couldn't find anything to stop the bleeding. I had to keep moving. I didn't know when the men would come back and find me. I don't remember the walk towards the building, but I prayed, prayed that God would lead me where I needed to go, to where I would be safe. The last thing I remember is walking into long grass and thinking I can't go on. That I couldn't walk any further. I don't remember anything until I woke up here." She looked up at him and nodded.

"That's good, Fynn. Now, can you describe the men?"

"I can. If you can find me a pad of paper and a pen, I can do a sketch of them."

Dallas held up his hand. "I'll have a police artist come out tomorrow. She'll do the sketch for you."

"Of course. I wasn't thinking, now was I?" Fynn was angry, angry that she had been hurt, angry that she had lost a week of time when she wanted to be doing something else, angry that she had been taken captive and threatened. "He threatened me, threatened Brady, threatened the men and ladies here. How do I stay, Dallas?"

"You stay because this is where you will be safe, as long as you stay close to the building. You stay because this is your home. You stay because a certain male I know wants you to."

"Male?" Her brow wrinkled as she puzzled that out. "Eric doesn't live here. He would want me to stay but he would leave the decision to me."

"It's not Eric that I'm thinking of. It's Brady. It went hard with him this week when you were gone."

She frowned again. "Brady? He shouldn't have been like that. I'm not that important to him. I mean, he's a friend and all that." Her words died away as Dallas simply smiled and shook his head. "Dallas?"

"It's more than that with him, Fynn. In case you missed it, he cares deeply for you. He would spend hours searching for you, praying to find you. You're the most important person in his life, I would suspect."

"I can't be." Her voice was barely above a whisper, even as hope rose in her heart, that just maybe God had been behind this all, that God had provided her the knight she had prayed for all her life. The knight that was never wove into bedtime stories just because her mother or father never told her bedtime stories. Those were reserved for the times she spent staying overnight at her aunt's. Those were the cherished memories she had.

"He's your knight." Dallas almost seemed to read her mind. "And his new truck is white." He didn't look up at her as he packed away his laptop, a smile hidden from her, but he heard her gasp and then her quiet prayer, a prayer he didn't think that she realized she was breathing aloud. "I'm out of here. I'll have more questions over the next few days for you. If you think of anything, call me or call Will. He can send someone out to talk with you."

Dallas paused outside her door, his eyes on the floor, his heart heavy knowing that he was no further ahead in the search. The man she described as her captor? They had found a body matching his description this morning in the downtown area. The responding officers had informed Dallas that the man had been described as being intoxicated and because of that had lost his balance on a balcony and fallen to his death. He would find a picture of him and show it to her, he thought. Now, the youth? What was that about, he wondered?

Brady moved closed to Dallas, his head tilted at he studied his friend.

"Dallas?"

Dallas shook his head to clear his thoughts, even as he raised it to answer Brady. "You can go back in. She's given me her statement. I'll need to have her read it over and sign it in the next hour or so. Don't be asking her any questions or letting her talk about it."

"I won't. Thank you." Brady moved past him, the door closing behind him even as Cadee walked towards Dallas.

"Dallas?"

"She's hurting, Cadee. Brady will help, but you four ladies? You have experienced something similar. Talk to her. Be honest with her. I know you and Benen were married when you went through what you did." Dallas paused, his head turning so that he could eye the door. "Somehow, I think those two will marry before this is all over."

"I think you may be right, Dallas. Only time and God will tell us."

Chapter 19

A week later, Fynn stared at Brady, in shock at his words, before she spun and ran from him, her hands hitting the lobby door and flying open from the force of her shove. She stopped and stared over her shoulder before she turned, heading for the garden that had become her favourite, the ones with all the daisies, columbines, and coneflowers. She loved to sit and watch the butterflies and bees as they hovered over the flowers. Fynn dropped to a bench, her face covered with her hands as she willed back the tears, a few falling that she could not stop. Brady was hovering and she couldn't have that. In fact, she wasn't used to it, and while she could see and understand his concern, she didn't like feeling trapped. Not unless there was a deeper meaning to his concern, and that he had not said.

Brady stared after her, his hands clasped on the top of his head. He hadn't mean to scare her or chase her away with his words. He had simply asked her to go out to dinner with him, and that he wanted to talk to her about where they were headed, if they were heading anywhere at all as a couple. He headed after her almost on a run, but stopped short, almost knocking Buckley down as he appeared in his path.

"Brady?" Buckley's voice held a touch of amusement. "Chasing someone down, are you?"

Brady smirked. "I was, until someone jumped into my way. Buckley?"

"Do I need to talk to her for you? I can, you know." Buckley's hand on Brady's shoulder moved him forward. "I gather you're trying to talk to her, and she didn't like it."

"No, I don't think that's it." Brady sighed, his hands scrubbing down his cheeks. He had come home from work, a long, hot, heartbreaking day with fatalities in the accidents they had responded to, and after he had cleaned up, the only thing he had any desire to do was to take Fynn out to dinner and for a long walk along the boardwalk that ran the shoreline in the town.

"She's scared, Brady. We've talked, her and I. She didn't have that great an upbringing. She told me her parents were distant, that she could never please them no matter how hard she tried or what she accomplished or won. She didn't understand it growing up, but now that she has remembered her brother and after speaking with her aunt and uncle, she thinks that her parents withdrew because of that."

"I think she's right, but it doesn't help now." Brady's steps slowed as he watched Fynn, huddled over, her face still buried in her hands. "How do I reach her, Buckley? How do I help her to heal?"

"By being there for her. By praying for her. By encouraging her. Barnabas would say that is crucial to your relationship, you encouraging her. That's what this Foundation is about. You've watched us all at times doing this, particularly our four friends who are now married. She needs to heal, and a big part of helping that is for you to do just what I said. Encourage her to talk, to seek help when she needs it. She's rootless right now. Her work was her life, and she has stepped back from that."

"It was, and she has. She told me she wants to set up a lab somewhere to study the insects here more fully, but she doesn't have the money to do that. She understands that the Foundation would help her, as her research would and could be used in fighting crime."

"That it would." Buckley watched as Fynn's head raised as she realized she was not on her own. "She knows you're here, Brady. I'll let you two talk."

Brady's hand on his arm stopped Buckley in his tracks. "No, please stay. I need to ask Fynn some questions and I would like our pastor to be in on that." He gave a small smile. "And as a friend, but mostly as our pastor. I need guidance and advice."

Buckley nodded, having a feeling in his heart where this was going. "First, has Dallas said if they are any further ahead in their investigation?"

Brady shrugged, at a loss in that. "He said the vagrant they found dead was the man who abducted her. They have tied him to Tyler Oakes."

"Tyler? He's the one, then. The youth she talked about. I've worried about him. He's always been hard, but he has a good heart underneath. If we can find him before he comes of age, maybe we can reach him."

"I think you have, Buckley. I have watched him study you and try to do what you're doing."

"He has? I'll put the word out that I need to talk to him. Don't worry. I won't push him."

Fynn watched as Brady and Buckley stood talking before she rose and approached him, ducking under the arm Brady raised to draw her to his side

"Guys? You seem deep in conversation. I don't want to intrude."

"Never intruding. I'm here as your pastor and friend, Fynn. Brady tells me that he needs to talk with you." Buckley grinned at the glare tossed his way.

"I do, Fynn. I really wanted to take you out to dinner and for a walk, but let's sit. I need to explain myself better. I'm not good with words the way Burnie, our author, is."

Fynn sat, Brady's arm still around her to tuck her close to him. "Okay. You wanted to talk?"

"First, Brady, Fynn. Let's pray. God is here but we need to ask for His guidance in this conversation." Buckley's head went down and he was praying before either one of the others could respond.

Brady gave a quiet word of thanks when Buckley finished. He knew that whatever Fynn was facing was not over, not by a long shot as his father would have said. He studied the ground, his shoe moving over the grass. He felt Fynn's hand on his, her grasp light but reassuring.

Looking up, Brady studied the beautiful lady in front of him, thankful for her and how she challenged him, grateful for the courage she showed, but unsure how to really say what he needed to say. His mouth opened and closed a few times before he caught the gleam of mischief and teasing in Fynn's eyes.

"Fynn. We haven't known each other that long, but I feel that I know you better than anyone I've known for years." He groaned as she laughed at him. "That's not how I meant to say that. What I mean is that I love you, love you more than I ever thought I could. I want to explore our friendship, to see where it goes, to see if you would be willing to be the missing part of my heart, the helpmeet God has sent for me."

"Explore our friendship, you say?" Fynn was enjoying herself teasing him, seeing him tense at her words. "Brady?" When he didn't look at her, her hand reached to his face, to turn it towards her. "Don't you see? Others have. You are the missing part of my heart, the one I didn't know I needed. I love you as well." She turned as she heard a choked sound from Buckley, her puzzlement turning to a glare. "Buckley, behave yourself."

"I'm sorry. It's just that we've all seen this since you arrived, Fynn. We just couldn't figure out how you two were missing this." His grin said he was enjoying himself, even as he prayed for them.

"We weren't missing it, Buckley. God hadn't prepared our hearts yet. But now He has." Fynn turned back, missing Buckley's nod at her wisdom. "So, Brady, what do you say? Will you marry me? Grow old with me? Serve God as He would direct us?"

Chapter 20

His heart pounding and his whole body shaking, Brady stared at Fynn, not quite sure that she was serious, but he could see she was. He saw the glimmer of tears in her eyes and knew that she had put herself out of her comfort zone to ask him that very question. He reached to draw her close, his arms wrapping around her, his head down on hers. He didn't hear Buckley's quiet words of prayer for them.

He leaned back, his eyes meeting Fynn's before he grinned. "What will we tell our children, darlin'? That you asked me to marry you?"

"Brady!" Fynn's cry of disbelief hit him in his heart.

"I agree, darlin'. I will marry you. Buckley, be quiet."

Buckley had begun to laugh, although he had tried to choke it back. "You two are just too funny for words, did you know that? I would be pleased to explain it to your children, if God so blesses. Let me pray for you, and then I'll disappear. This moment is for you two alone. Come see me to set a day, although I do have this Saturday available."

The couple could hear Buckley's chuckle as he waved as he walked away, before they turned to each other.

"Did I really ask that?" Fynn was dismayed. It should have been Brady.

"You did. Now, let me ask you a question. Will you be mine, Fynn, mine to cherish and love and grow old with, to serve God as we should, to be that blessing to others that He would have us be?"

She nodded before she was swept into his arms. When she could breathe again, she looked up at him, content for the moment, but still worried.

"But what about the men after me? What happens with them?"

"We can worry about the all we want, but it won't find them. We'll leave it for Dallas and his teammates to find them." He sat back, his arms around his love. "When?"

Fynn began to giggle, something he had not heard from her before. "Buckley did say he had time this Saturday, didn't he?" When Brady began to laugh, she smirked. "I don't want to rush it, but I don't want to wait too long." She sighed, bringing his eyes to her. "Mom and Dad are away for a month. I'll send them a text, but I don't think they'll care."

"We will wait if they want us to. If not, we can do a virtual ceremony with them, if they want."

Fynn nodded, rising when Brady stood, taking the hand he held out for her, a shiver running through her as she feared for his life. She remembered the threats that had been lodged against him. How did she do it, Lord? How do I do it? How do I keep him safe? She searched the area around them as they walked slowly back towards the building, not seeing the youth who had been her captor standing in the shadows, watchful, his eyes searching for anyone who would find him. He finally turned and walked away, his shoulders slumped. To see them together had not been what he had hoped for. He knew Buckley was wanting to speak with him and he had a good idea what it was about. He had been avoiding him and would continue to do that. He would also need to avoid the men who had hired him. Suddenly, Toronto or even Ottawa or the Maritimes seemed like a wonderful place to live.

Brady stopped suddenly, a hand rubbing at his face. Fynn stared up at him, not sure what had happened.

"We need to talk, Fynn. I don't think that it has been explained to you what happens when we fellows marry."

She nodded. "The ladies did. I would expect to receive a salary,wouldn't I?"

Brady nodded, his eyes searching her. "You will. But more than that. Barnabas caught me when I got home today. He's wanting to speak with you. He's talked to his Dad and the other board members. They want to offer you the funds to set up a research facility for your bugs and insects. He's hoping you will say yes. He's looking far into the future, but his Dad mentioned that you could become a training facility for entomologists, using your forensics experience that way."

Fynn stared at him, her eyes huge, her mouth in a circle. "How did they know?" Her voice was barely audible.

"Know what, darlin'?" Brady hugged her, waiting for her to speak.

"That's my dream, you know. I had a vision of myself doing just that before I graduated. Thank you."

"No, the thanks go to Barnabas and the board. Now, let's head into town. I want to take my sweetheart out for a meal."

Neither saw Barnabas standing in the parking lot, his hand raised to flag them down. Buckley stood beside him, a smirk on his face.

"They only have eyes for each other tonight, you know"

"I can see that. Know something you want to share?" Barnabas grinned at him.

"Nope. It's theirs for the telling."

"Like that, is it? I can wait. If you see Brady or Fynn, let them know I want to talk to them, sooner rather than later."

"I will. Listen, I talked to Dallas today. He was looking for the youth."

"And?" Barnabas waited, his eyes on the keys he held in his hand.

"They can't find him but the word on the street is that someone is looking for Fynn and means to find her. Knowing she's connected here, the street people are staying silent."

"That's good. Send out word that meals and what they need will be available through the shelter or the diner." Barnabas walked away, his words echoing in Buckley's ears. It wasn't the first time the Foundation had done that.

"I will, Barnabas. I will. But I fear for Fynn and now for Brady. It's not over for them, not by a long shot." Buckley stared towards the road before he too turned and walked away, not seeing

Blair and Devaney watching him before they exchanged glances and both shrugged.

Chapter 21

A week later, Fynn shoved her feet into her hiking boots, tied them, and then stood, her hand reaching for the cotton shirt she had set ready to don. She was heading out to research the area, but fear held her back. She shrugged. What can happen that hasn't already happened, she thought. I can do this. I have to, don't I, Lord? I can't hide or live in fear. I just ask that You protect Brady. I can't live with myself if he is hurt once more. Fynn paused, a thought crossing her mind. Was someone different after Brady? Was it connected to her only or to him as well? She shrugged, her hand reaching for the backpack she had left handy.

Shutting and locking her door, Fynn headed for the lobby, stopping in surprise as she saw Brady as well as Bradon and Ennis waiting for her, all dressed in casual clothing that said they were ready for a hike.

"Brady?" Fynn walked slowly towards him, a puzzled look on her face at his grin.

"I had the day off. Unexpected. To make up for some shifts I've picked up. Bradon and Ennis were free as well. We would like to join you on your hike, if we may. If you say no, we'll just head in the same direction but stay behind you." He continued to grin at her frown, hearing Bradon's chuckle and Ennis' laughing comment to behave himself.

Fynn shrugged. "I guess. It's not exciting for anyone else. Most people don't like my creepy-crawlies."

"I, for one, would enjoy it greatly. I have always been fascinated with certain bugs, but have had no one to talk to me about them." Ennis linked her arm through Fynn's and drew her outside. "So, tell me. How do we go about this? Do you gather them into containers or just watch them?

Fynn laughed, her heart suddenly free of the restrictions she had always felt. She had been an anomaly in her family. She knew her mother didn't like her line of work at all and her father had bluntly told her to find something else to do. She had stared at him that day, watched him walk away from her in anger, and knew in her heart that she just would never please them, no matter what she did.

"I plan on doing both. You can help."

"Great!" Ennis' smile lit up her face. "Talk to me, Fynn. Tell me about your work."

Fynn did just that, explaining how she took samples of eggs, larvae, and bugs or insects from a crime scene and then analyzed them, determining their ages and if they were resident to the area.

"Wow! I didn't realize it was so involved." Bradon's voice had Fynn's head snapping around, surprise on her face. "I'm sorry. I wasn't meaning to eavesdrop but this is fascinating. Have you ever considered lecturing on this?"

Fynn shrugged. "At one point, I had been asked to but refused. I couldn't face the people in my hometown with this. They would have shrugged it off as an obsession I have had since a child."

"An obsession?" Brady shared a look with Bradon before he spoke again. "Not an obsession, Fynn. Not in the way they would mean. You have done a lot of good and brought healing to many through your work. I know you don't think of it that way, but God has given you knowledge and a talent that is rare to find."

Fynn blushed at his praise, not used to words such as his. "Thank you, love. Now, here's where I was hoping to work today."

Brady's hand on her arm stopped her. "Are you sure?"

She nodded, looking around the small meadow where she had been found. "I need to take this area back, Brady. If I don't, I can't heal and move on. I certainly would never be able to come this way again."

Brady nodded. "Then, that's what we do. We take it back for you. Bradon, a prayer to start, if you don't mind."

Hours later, flushed with laughter, Fynn sat back on the log she had found for a perch, a water bottle in her hand. She had never had so much fun, she thought. She had never taken time to make friends, to just be herself, the way Ennis was drawing her out. She missed Brady's speculative glance at her before he nodded.

"So, Fynn, now that we have been crawling around on our hands and knees chasing fast moving creatures, what do you do with them?" Bradon grinned at her as she made a face at him. He had come to appreciate the fine, dry sense of humour she had, dark at times, but he knew that came from her line of work. He saw it in Doc and Anna and in Brady.

"I take them home and preserve them. They will become the foundation of my work." She looked up suddenly, unsure of herself. "I just don't know if I can do this."

Brady's arm drew her close to him. "You can, darlin'. You can. This has been a dream of yours for years, hasn't it? Barnabas is wanting to talk to you again, didn't you say? He seems to have found land and an architect already."

"I know, and the speed of that scares me."

Ennis laughed. "Barnabas is a mover. He makes things happen. He doesn't throw his wealth around, asking for favouritism. People know that when he asks for something, it has been thought through thoroughly, and that he is ready to move. He has many friends and acquaintances who know him, know his character, know that the causes he picks up are near and dear to his heart, and that these are usually ones that will educate or enhance or bring about a change in someone's life, or in other words, bring change that is wanted or needed."

Brady nodded. "Ennis has said it well. That's what Barnabas wants. Even more, he wants to encourage people. He strives to be like Paul's companion, Barnabas. That's why he searched the country for men like us. He wanted to find ones who were on their own, that needed the encouragement he could offer. He also has said he was driven to find men with the same initials as his."

"Right there, that's what I don't get." Fynn sat forward, absentmindedly recapping her water bottle. "How did he find you all?"

Bradon shrugged, his thoughts going back to how he had been found by Barnabas, his heart grateful to the man who had become a good friend. "God. That's what he always says. He had investigators searching, presenting names. Barnabas would track us down, observe us, talk to people, and then offer us the position with the Foundation. His father has backed him all the way. Some of the board questioned at first what he was doing but they have all come around to thinking the same as he does." Bradon paused, his eyes on Ennis. "Even though we have gone through some pretty horrible things, he has stood beside us, not moving until we were safe. That's who he is."

Fynn nodded, a thoughtful look on her face. "I can see that, for the short time I have known him. Brady, we're not done yet. I talked to Dallas yesterday. He needs to sit down with us both in the next couple of days."

Chapter 22

Dallas studied the young couple in front of him, his eyes assessing them, not liking the strain that showed in both their faces. Lord, can we end this? They need this over. Fynn has healing to do that she can't while this is hanging over her head. They don't have to say anything but I know they have reached an agreement of some kind. They will tell us when they are ready, if and when he corrected himself.

"Dallas? Where do we stand in the investigation? It's seems to have gone on for so long." Fynn shook her head. "That's not fair. I know they things take time. I just so want this over."

"We do too, Fynn, for both your sakes." Dallas paused in his speech, looking down at his notes. "The man who abducted you? We are tracing him back, to your hometown in fact."

"That doesn't surprise me. Who is he connected to?" Fynn sat forward in her chair, intent on understanding what Dallas was or was not saying, depending on how you looked at it, she thought.

Brady watched her closely, seeing another side to her that he hadn't seen before, except so briefly that first day. "Fynn? What are you thinking? Or rather, who would you suspect?"

"The one you would suspect the least. Now, it could be the one you would suspect the most and set aside as being too obvious."

Dallas stared at her, amazed at how she had gotten right to the point.

"The latter, I think, Fynn. How well did you know the town treasurer?"

"Ted Langley? We went to school together but he was older than me. That was a given. I think he had failed a grade or two at the beginning of his school life. We could never figure out how he became the town treasurer. He was never good with math or numbers." Fynn rubbed at her temples, a headache starting to burn. "Are you saying that he's the one?"

Dallas shrugged. "We're looking at him. What else can you tell me about him? I have to make a trip up that way, but I would like to have more information on him. The townspeople I've talked to haven't been really forthcoming."

Fynn snorted, bringing a grin to Brady's sober face. "And they won't. The ones you would need to talk to won't talk to a stranger. They might talk to me, but I'm not the investigator. I don't think that they would talk with Eric even." Fynn rubbed at her face, distress showing. "Who can I send you to?"

"How about Eric's mother or his aunt?"

Fynn nodded, her eyes lighting up. "Perfect. His aunt has a B&B that you could stay at. That would be the perfect cover for you."

Dallas began to laugh. "You're reading too many cop novels, Fynn."

She stopped in her movement of raising her glass to her mouth to take a drink of juice, her eyes narrowing at him. "No, I don't read those. I don't read a lot, not any more, and I should. I need to go back to that." She set her glass down and moved away from the table, pacing before she was out of the room and then back, shoving one of her high school yearbooks at him. "Senior class. Read what he wrote about his life ambitions. I had forgotten what he had wrote." She shivered as she sat back down, her chair moved closer to Brady, who reached out to draw her close to him.

"Fynn?" Dallas raised his eyes. "Did he really say that? That he wanted to live life to the fullest and he really didn't care how he got to that?"

"He did. He was like that in school. We suspected he was behind the drugs and alcohol that used to appear at the parties. I never went but I heard rumours and stories. We think he was doing more that providing that."

"What are you thinking?" Dallas watched her closely as she shrugged.

"I am not really sure. There is someone else." She stared at the wall, a frown on her face, before the two men exchanged glances and then shrugged.

Dallas finally rose, taking Fynn's yearbook with him at her request. "Thanks for the information, Fynn. I'll be in touch."

Brady watched him walk away before he rose, gathering their dishes and washing them, waiting for Fynn to speak. When she didn't, he turned to lean against the counter, drying his hands on the small towel she kept draped over the over door handle.

"Fynn?" When she looked up, he drew in a deep breath at the devastation of her face. He was across the room, back in his chair, his arms reaching for her. "Fynn? What didn't you say?"

"I couldn't. I have no proof."

"Who, Fynn? Who do you suspect?"

She buried her face against him, and he felt the sobs shaking her body. His head rested on hers as he prayed for her, bringing her to the throne, asking for healing for her.

Fynn finally just rested against him. "I don't have proof."

"And you don't want to accuse anyone without it. But, who, Fynn?" He waited before he finally spoke a name.

Fynn stilled even more. "How did you guess?"

Brady shrugged. "It just makes sense. Now, we have to prove it. I know the guys will want in on it."

Fynn sat back, her eyes on him. "I have a contact I can reach out to. She's good at what she does. She'll look into it without anyone knowing. I have no idea how she does what she does but she is so good at it. She has resources even the biggest police department doesn't have."

"Okay, let's do that. But for now, where's your Bible? We need to find verses to live by."

She rose, a hand reaching out for his, and headed to the living room, curling up on the couch as Brady lifted her Bible from the end table where she had left it. She listened as he read through numerous verses, her heartache easing, her mind beginning to slow. Thank you, Lord, she breathed, for. bringing Brady into my life. He's what I need, and You knew and planned for it.

Chapter 23

Barnabas hesitated the next day as he walked towards his vehicle, a frown on his face for a moment. I should know this couple, but I'm not sure that I do. The lady, and it was a lady, he decided, not just a woman, walked towards him.

"Good morning. Do you know where I can find Fynn? I need to speak with her." Her voice was low and melodious.

The man with her reached for Barnabas' outstretched hand. "You are Barnabas Carey. We met years ago.'

The name finally came to Barnabas.

"Abe Finlay. And this must be Emma."

"That would be me." Emma looked past him, before she moved away, without excusing herself.

Abe grinned. "Sorry. She can have a one-track mind at times. I would suspect that she has found Fynn."

Barnabas spun. "And she has. And all my guys as well." Barnabas grinned at Abe. "Where are your guys?"

"They all wanted to come. Don't be surprised if they all show up at some point. They know of Fynn. Know her work. She helped solve a case for a friend of ours back a couple of years. They have not forgotten that. They said to tell you that they will help in any way they can."

The two men approached Emma and Fynn, Brady standing with an arm around her, the other twelve men and the four ladies circling them. Emma and Fynn were in deep discussion.

Abe looked around, feeling uncomfortable.

"Can we go somewhere inside, Barnabas? Someone's out here."

Barnabas nodded and then spoke to the group, directing them inside. "Thanks, Abe. I think we'll need to have a talk with Fynn.

She has no fear, or hides it well. She's out and about, without any concern for her safety."

"No, she's concerned. She's hiding her fear and concern from you. She doesn't want to worry any of you and certainly does not want to put any of you in danger. But she has, just by doing that very thing."

Barnabas stared at him for a moment, not quite sure Abe had read Fynn right. He turned as he heard a throat clearing beside him.

Brady stood there, his eyes on Fynn as she moved away with Emma, the other four ladies with them, his friends following, their eyes watchful.

"Abe's right, Barnabas. She tries to hide how she's feeling. She has felt for years that no one listens to her, that no one really cares what happens to her. Eric, now there, she has been freer with him than with others and with her aunt and uncle. But that's because Eric pushes her. I've heard their discussions, full voice at times." He grinned at the astonished look on Barnabas' face. "Didn't expect that, did you?" He paused, a thoughtful look on his face. "What she went through when she was abducted? That is changing her. Coming here, away from her hometown? She is uncertain if she should have. She's trying to find her way, to heal from the past and whatever hurts she has not yet shared with me."

Abe's hand was in the air as he waved it to stop Brady's words. "Just a moment. Did you say she was abducted?"

"She was. She was gone for a week. She made her way back towards here. The only thing they asked of her was where a man was. She has no idea who." Brady paused, his face hardening. "Did you know that she has a brother who disappeared when she was two?"

Abe stared at him before he spun to stare after Emma. "That must be what she meant." He walked rapidly towards the building.

"What who meant?" Brady ran to catch up with him, Barnabas torn between where he needed to be and where he wanted to be before he headed to his vehicle and drove away. He would catch up with them later.

"Emma. She was muttered something about a man named Flannery."

Brady held the door open for Abe and then pointed towards a hallway. "They'll be in the conference room. And yes, Flannery is Fynn's brother. She had forgotten him, driven her childhood memories deep inside. She's tried so hard over her lifetime to please her parents, but hasn't been able to reach through to them."

"A friend of ours who is a psychologist would say that she did that to protect herself. Repressing her memories." Abe sighed as he stood just inside the conference room doorway, his eyes wandering over all the people in there, watching as they had scattered to work. Emma stood beside Benen, deep in conference. "The man Emma's talking to?"

"Benen? He's an IT guy."

"She finds them, somehow. She has her employees working on this. She wants this over for Fynn."

"How did they meet?" Brady watched his lady, seeing her ruffled curls where she had drawn her hands through them, her attention focused on Brendon as he spoke with her.

"Fynn was instrumental in solving a case that involved close friends of ours. The man had disappeared and we searched for him. Fynn was brought in as an expert witness, having done what she does best, finding the evidence that proved when he was killed. It saved his son from being charged."

"Wow! I knew she was good."

Abe grinned. "And when's the wedding?" He laughed as Brady stared at him, finally remembering to snap his mouth closed. "All my guys on my team, Emma and I, and a number of close friends have had what we call adventures, sometimes to the point of being life threatening."

"Sounds like four of my friends. We almost lost Bradon and Ennis." Brady finally walked towards Fynn, his hands resting on her shoulders.

Fynn tilted her head to look up at him, silent communication between them, before she went back to the papers in front of her.

"Fynn? Talk to me." Brady slid into a chair beside her, exchanging a look with Brendon.

Fynn looked up, a devastated look on her face. "This! How did Emma ever find this?"

Chapter 24

Finally, Emma rose from the computer she had been using, her eyes on Abe as he nodded. She approached Fynn, sitting beside her, an arm around her.

"Fynn. We need to be leaving. We'll come back if you need us to. Call me. I'll send what I have found to the detective, Dallas, is it?"

Fynn nodded, a sad look on her face. "Thank you, my friend. I am glad you have found Flannery. Or at least, I think you have. He's nearby, isn't he?"

Emma nodded. "That's what we have determined. He is likely watching for you. We have found his foster parents. He was never adopted, and no one knows why. He would be able to tell you. Jace has traced his travels in the last few months. He has been back to your hometown."

"He has? Is he the one I've felt watching me?" Hope rose in Fynn's heart. She desperately wanted to meet the brother that she could only vaguely remember.

"We suspect so. Call me, Fynn, even if you just need to talk. You know my story."

"I do." She looked past Emma at Brady, who stood nearby, deep in conversation with Burnie. "May I share it with Brady?"

"That you can. If you need to talk to any one of us ladies, call us. The guys are worried about you. If they hadn't had to be training today, they would have all come."

Fynn started to laugh, Emma grinning with her. "I can see that. Other than the seven, how many others would have come?"

Emma laughed. "You know us too well. Listen, when you get your facility up and running, call us. We want a tour. And I know Joseph will want to do your security system."

Fynn shook her head. "Tell him Brady has a friend, Branigan, who is as good as he is. A little healthy competition there won't hurt."

Emma laughed. "You know them well." She rose, a final hug given and then she walked away.

Brady stood for a moment before he approached Fynn.

"You okay?" He enveloped her in his arms, his chin on the top of her head.

"I am, thank you." She moved so she could look up at him. "Emma says Flannery was back in our hometown."

"I am sure he has been. He's trying to figure out how to approach you, without putting you in danger. Or any more danger than you have been in."

"Do you think so?" Fynn sighed, the sigh seemingly drawn up from the very tips of her toes.

"Now what, Fynn? Are you at a point you can leave it for today?"

Fynn leaned past him to study the table, seeing the untidy mess of papers, and frowned. "I don't work like that. I don't have messy piles of papers." She turned as she heard laughter.

Bradon was grinning at her even as Baird was laughing.

"I would say you did this time. Let me tidy it up for you and then we can lock it away in the safe. We'll let you set your own combination and then you can access it whenever you want. I feel like I'm going to tell you something you already know, but don't bury yourself in here or under the paperwork. Understand, please, that we all will be working on it. Dallas has copies, I just spoke with him. You need to keep your strength up, Fynn, and I suspect you won't do that unless we set boundaries on you."

She frowned at him, anger flaring for a moment, her mouth opening to speak before Brady's arms tightened around her.

She nodded. "I know that, Bradon. I really do. It's just that......"Her voice died away before she broke away from Brady and ran, tears that she wasn't even aware she was shedding glistening on her cheeks.

Brady stood for a moment, his eyes following her, his hand rubbing at his face. He finally turned to his two friends, not seeing the others gathering around them.

"I'm sorry, Bradon. I don't know what to say."

Bradon shrugged. "It's okay. She's been due to break. I thought it would have happened earlier.'

Brady shook his head, finally seeing his friends surrounding him. "It's just that Emma confirmed her brother has been here in town, likely looking for her, and then back in her hometown." He listened to the murmurs from the men. "She doesn't remember him, and that hurts her. It hurts her too how her parents are reacting and haven't even been in touch since she moved down here." He could feel anger building and struggled to control it. "Do you know that they left town when she was abducted, sometime during that week. They never bothered to even call Eric to see what they could do, or to see if Fynn had been found. That cuts deep. It just gives her more to heal from. And how do I encourage her to heal with that hanging over us?" He stopped speaking, his mouth opening as if he wanted to say something else before he shook his head and walked away rapidly, heading in the opposite direction that Fynn had. He needed air and a chance to clear his mind and let his emotions settle. He did need to talk to Barnabas but that would wait until the next day.

Chapter 25

Shutting his apartment door, Brady walked towards his office, sinking down in the chair, his head going down on his hands as his elbows rested on the desk. He was discouraged, down in the dumps, he thought, to use a phrase of his mother's. Lord, I am not sure anymore. Not sure where I'm heading. I love my career, my volunteer work at the shelter, my life here. Even now with Fynn, Lord, how I love that lady, but it seems that I am waiting for something, something that's about to happen, and I have to admit that scares me.

He raised his head, a bleak look on his face as he stared across the room. He ignored the vibrating of his phone. He needed to, he thought, before he rose, heading for the outdoors, his head bent as he walked, hands shoved into his jeans' pockets. He didn't see Brennen watching him and then following after him, concern colouring his face.

Brady finally stopped at the lake, his feet sinking into the sand, before he walked towards a rock pile, perching himself on one and staring out at the lake. He was watching the waves moving towards the shore, nor the seagulls wheeling in the air. He ignored their harsh calls.

He finally stood, his head down for a moment before he raised it, determination on it and in his walk as he headed back for the building. He paused as he saw a man standing in his way, a younger man he thought, around his own age. His steps slowed before he finally paused.

"Can I help you? You are on private property."

The man nodded. "I know. You're Brady? If you are, we need to talk."

"Maybe. I need to know who you are. Let's see some identifications."

The other man gave a quick grin before he pulled out his wallet and tossed it at Brady, whose hands came up instinctively to catch it.

Brady watched the man closely before he glanced down at the wallet, opening it and pulling out the driver's license. Shock waved through him and he glanced up quickly, to find the man nodding.

"Please, don't say my name out loud." He paused as his hand reached for the wallet. "I just wanted to find you, to let you know I am around." He spun on his heel and was gone before Brady could speak.

Finding Barnabas on the patio at the back of the building, Breck approached, to drop down in the chair beside him, his head going back as his eyes slid shut. He breathed deeply, feeling that he needed to clear both his mind and his lungs. He felt the warmth from the rays of the setting sun on him and heard the sounds of dusk, the daytime creatures settling down as the nighttime creatures were awakening. It was a favourite time of day for him, a time just to sit and meditate, letting his favourite Scriptures run through his mind before he bowed his head to pray. That wasn't happening tonight.

"Breck?" Barnabas' voice finally broke through the silence between them. "You're burdened heavily tonight."

Breck nodded, without opening his eyes, a look of concern and then sorrow crossing his face. "I am. I think of Fynn and how her family have treated her. That would make good fodder for a psychiatrist."

"It would. Unfortunately, all we can do is pray for that.. But there is more." Barnabas watched his friend closely, knowing that Breck, who the men affectionately called the boss' stand-in, took his responsibilities seriously, and prayerfully. If he is that burdened, Lord, there is something there that we have missed or thought of lesser importance.

Breck raised his head, his eyes opening before he turned to his friend. "There is. There is something off about this whole thing. I think Fynn knows who is behind it and is denying it. I want to look closer at that lab she worked in. I know it's well thought of but there is something not ringing true."

"Abe mentioned that. He said Emma was looking into all of the men and women who worked there. If Fynn had found her lab and office searched, then someone wanted something from her or was doing it to scare her."

"That's my take." Breck looked up, one eye closing against the sunset, to find Brady and Burnie standing in front of them. "Brady? I don't like the look on your face."

Brady gave a grim nod even as he sat on the bench in front of the two, Burnie dropping down beside him. "I'm not happy. I am more worried about Fynn than before." He exchanged a look with Burnie. "I went for a walk to the lake. On my way back, I was approached by a man. I have no idea where he came from or disappeared to, but he showed me his identification." He paused, still not quite sure of who he had met.

"And?" When Brady didn't answer Breck's question, he asked again. "Brady? What aren't you telling us?"

"It was Fynn's brother. He didn't say what he wanted or even where he is staying. He stated he simply wanted to find me."

"That's bizarre. What did he actually want?" Barnabas leaned forward, his gaze moving between the two men.

"He didn't say." Burnie spoke. "I was near enough to hear the conversation. It's just as Brady said."

"We'll need to search the woods. Brady, you'll need to keep an eye out as you work. Whoever it is that seems to be after Flannery will be watching you as well, hoping you will lead them to him. He took a chance, meeting you like that."

Brady shrugged and then nodded. "I suppose. But who's after him and why? Why go after Fynn?"

"That's what we're working on. The guys have all said they're taking time, just like they did with Bradon, to work on this. Brody said Emma sending him a lot of information. In fact, she told him she'd be back in a couple of days."

"And bringing all those people with her?" Brady had to grin as he remembered the look on Fynn's face. "I don't know that Fynn could handle that."

The other three laughed, and then conversation turned to a new topic, the series of messages that Buckley was bringing, on how to be a blessing to others.

Chapter 26

Bradon was on a search. Ennis had heard from her father, that someone had been in their town, looking for Fynn, and had asked them to warn her. He would, he thought, if he could find her. He stood for a moment, eyeing the path to the lake, and then shook his head, searching instead through the parking lot before nodding. Her car was missing. But where was she? He ran for his own, heading into town, knowing he needed to find her, but not sure that he could.

Driving through the town he called home, he finally spotted Fynn's car. He pulled in and parked beside her, his eyes on the library. Was she there, Lord, or am I on a mission for nothing? He locked his door behind him, then paused. He should be talking to Brady, but Brady was on duty. Bradon shook his head, heading for the library, holding the door open for the two little children who scurried through and then held up the picture books they had in their hands, excitement emanating from them, their faces glowing. He grinned at them and then at their mother, who tried to apologize.

"Don't apologize." Bradon's words brought a smile to her own face. "I'm glad to see kids excited about reading."

He searched the library without finding Fynn. Where is she, Lord? Her car's here but she's not. I am not sure if she would have left it here and walked through the town. I don't know her well enough to make that kind of assessment.

Bradon turned as he heard his name call. Dallas was running towards him, a worried look on his face.

"Bradon? Where's Brady?"

"On duty. He's to be done at three but he figured it would go later. Why?"

Dallas held up a photo. "Do you know this man?"

Bradon took it, his eyes on Dallas before he looked down. "No, I'm not familiar with him. Should I be?"

Dallas shrugged. "His name has come up in our investigation. I need to speak with Fynn and Brady."

"I have a bad feeling, Dallas. I've been looking for Fynn and can't find her." Bradon turned, pointing to Fynn's car. "Her car's here but she's not in the library."

Dallas shot him a glance and then approached the vehicle. His hand on Bradon's chest stopped him in his tracks.

"Dallas?" Bradon's voice held confusion. He couldn't see the driver's side of the car, but Dallas could.

"Bradon, I need you to step back." Dallas' voice was grim as he spoke, a shuttered look coming over his face.

"Dallas, I can. But what's up?"

"What's up? There's blood on the side of her car, and I suspect that's her purse there."

Bradon's eyes slid shut as his heart fell. "She's been taken again. Is that what you're saying?"

Dallas nodded. "That's my fear." He turned, pointing to the bench under the spreading red oak tree on the library lawn. "Sit over there. I'll need to talk to you."

It was only noon when Dallas finally approached Bradon, sinking down with a sigh. He was weary, he thought, too many cases and not enough time. He thought coming on the force here and then moving up so quickly to detective would be an easier life for him. It hadn't happened that way.

"Dallas?" Bradon's voice broke into his thoughts.

"Whoever it was, they've been injured. We're not sure if it's Fynn, but with her purse there, we suspect it was." He looked down at the photo he had retrieved. "The word we had was that this man was looking for her. I pray he didn't find her." His head raised as he heard a yell and then he was up and running towards the officer heading his way, Bradon on his heels.

"Dallas? Someone saw Dr. Daley shoved into a vehicle and managed to snap a photo of the vehicle and the plate. We've found the vehicle, abandoned in the woods near the Foundation building."

The officer paused to catch his breath. "Will is sending a team out there now."

Dallas spun, heading for his own vehicle. "Bradon, after me. Head for the Foundation. The guys who are there right now will want to know. But we can't have you out there, not yet. Not until we know for sure that's where she's likely to be."

Bradon nodded. "On my way. I pray it's not Brady who gets the call."

Dallas spun, horror briefly on his face before he shuttered it. "Pray that way, but it's a toss up if he does or not."

Dallas approached the vehicle shortly thereafter, a frown on his face. He remembered seeing the vehicle around town, the out-of-province license plate a giveaway that whoever it was didn't belong there. He turned as an officer approached.

"We've run the plates, Dallas. It was stolen three weeks ago from British Columbia."

"Three weeks? Any sense of who?"

The officer shook his head. "No, there isn't. Not surprisingly." He turned, looking towards the trees. "We're searching. The K-9s are here and headed in. Will's pulled in whoever he can to search."

Dallas nodded, walking towards the vehicle. "I've seen this car around town but never got a good look at the driver. I wish I had. I had no reason to suspect it wasn't on the up and up."

"None of us did. Dr. Daley? Is that who you suspect is involved?"

"I think so." Dallas ducked to look through the driver's window. "Her purse was found beside her car and there is some blood on the door. Look, there are folders and what looks like documents on the seat. Whoever it is was either sloppy or planned to return. Find some officers and start searching for the man."

"Man?"

"I would suspect so. Fynn wouldn't go with a woman, not if she could help it. I see a man's jacket and hat on the backseat."

Dallas turned as he heard running footsteps and then ran towards the path, meeting a female officer running his way.

"Alice?"

"We found her, but we're not approaching her. Something is off. Will is there. He's asked for the ERT and bomb squads."

"ERT? Bomb squad?" Dallas paled, his face growing stern, before he was past Alice and on the run for Will.

"Dallas?" Will turned partway to speak.

"Fynn? Alice said they found her."

Will was grim. "They have but we need to send in the right people. I have a call in for the paramedics as well."

"Let's pray it's not Brady, but those teams have been extra busy for some reason today."

Will nodded. "That was my request, but dispatch said they'd send whoever was free, even if it was Brady. What's your sense of what's going on with those two?"

"I would say they're engaged or close to it."

They waited, stress building as first the ERT and then the bomb squad members passed them. Finally the ERT leader returned, his face pale, sweat beading his forehead.

"Will? We have a huge problem."

"Robert? Explain, please."

"It's Dr. Daley but we can't move her right now. She's alive, has a knife wound on her side, but that's not the issue."

"And the issue would be?" Will waited for a moment as Robert composed himself.

"She said she's laying on something and that if she moves, it will inject her with a drug of some kind."

"What?" Will's exclamation expelled from. "Now what?"

"Theodore's working on a solution, but it's Dr. Daley. It's like she has given up and is resigned to dying."

Chapter 27

That morning, Fynn had risen early, just as the sun was rising, and grabbing her Bible, had headed for the balcony of her apartment. She had spent time searching for verses that would encourage her. She was discouraged, she thought, and that was not her. She could usually look on the bright side of life, but the last few months, work had drained her. She had been driven from her home by someone unknown, she had left the only town she had ever really gotten to know. Fynn sighed as she thought of her parents. Where are they, Lord? Why is there no contact? I just need my Mom and she's not there for me. I can't go to my aunt, not and endanger her. Eric is near but our relationship is changing, now that I'm dating. He's stepping back as my protector, letting Brady take over.

Fynn's face softened and her eyes grew wistful as she thought of Brady. I know he's the one, Lord, the one You mean for me, but I don't want him hurt. Buckley would tell me to trust, we've had some good talks, he and I, but it's so hard when I feel something hanging over me, something that may well endanger my love.

She grinned to herself as she remembered the look on Brady's face the night she proposed and then the look on his face as he proposed to her himself. He has such a dry sense of humour. I'm glad he takes pleasure in what he does.

She finally rose, setting her Bible back on the end table in the living room before she reached for her purse. She needed to get out, to get to know her town. A stop at the library was in order, she decided, a place she could lose herself for hours if she knew herself.

Fynn walked towards her car a couple of hours later, keys in her hand, her thoughts on the welcome she had found in the building behind her. She smiled, knowing that she had found somewhere she could live and work and yes, marry and raise a family, if that was God's will for her. She didn't see the man approaching her until she was shoved against her car, a small scream torn from her, her keys and purse falling to the pavement. She felt the slice of the knife as it hit her side.

"Dr. Daley. You're a hard person to find on your own. This must be my lucky day." The man's voice was hoarse, a smoker, she decided, and wheezy.

"Please? Let me go. I don't have anything you want."

Fynn was afraid as she slumped against the car, her hand on her side, eyes wide as she studied the man in front of her. It was difficult to see his face, the hood on his sweatshirt pulled up and as far forward as he could get it. She didn't think she knew him, but she feared. She was in his hands, literally as he roughly pulled her away from her own vehicle, her bloodied hand brushing against the door, and shoved her towards his own vehicle. The trunk was popped open, and after glancing around, he shoved her into it, binding her hands.

Darkness descended as the lid slammed shut. Where are You, Lord, she murmured. Do You know where I am? Do You care? Her unspoken prayer was one of desperation and despair.

She felt the car moving, picking up speed for a bit before it slowed and she felt it turning, the ride becoming bumpy. The car stopped and she felt it shift as the man slid out. Fynn prayed, fear rising within her, in a lady who really didn't fear. This was out of what she had ever expected she'd ever face. In her work, she had gone into scenes and sites that made men cringe, but she had always felt safe, knowing there were officers around. This time, she was on her own.

The trunk lid opened and she was pulled out as roughly as she was shoved into it. She took a moment to find her balance, wanting to reach for her side, but prevented from doing so. The man muttered to himself before he dragged her away from the car, turned her to face the woods, and then hand on her back, shoved her forward. She stumbled as she walked, unable to find the balance that she needed, knowing that the fear and pain was driving that from her.

A hand on her arm stopped Fynn's forward step. She stared around the small clearing, fear once more rising harder and higher.

"Over there." The man pointed with his knife and Fynn cringed back, not moving. He muttered something, cursed and then dragged her forward, stopping in the centre of the clearing, his eyes on the ground and then searching the area around. He had scoped out that very clearing for the task he had been given. That it was a woman he had been tasked to kill made no difference to him. It would not be the first time he had done that very deed.

"On the ground." His harsh voice thundered at her.

Fynn froze, her eyes on him and then the ground, her head beginning to shake even as she tried to move away from him.

"On the ground." He shoved her forward and then down.

The pain from hitting her side with the stab wound rushed through her and Fynn bit at her lip to stop her cries from sounding. She felt his hands on her, positioning her on her side, even as blackness welled in front of her. She blinked, watching as the knife approached and then sliced at the bond holding her hands together.

Fynn shuddered, not knowing what was coming. The man stood and watched her, finally speaking.

"Don't move, unless you want to die."

"What?" Fynn's voice was getting weak. "What do you mean?"

"I mean, little lady, that you don't move. You're are laying on a container that if you move, a syringe will pop up and inject you with a drug. Enough drug to kill you quickly." He cackled as he saw the look of horror cross her face and her lips trembling before she bit at them.

"Like I said, don't move. I'll just leave you here. I am sure the bugs you study will find you."

He cackled once more, pulled out a cigarette, looked at it before he stuffed it into his mouth, and then spun on his heel to walk away, leaving Fynn on the ground, terror on her face, tears she didn't know she was shedding dripping from her cheek to land on the ground.

Fynn had no doubt that he had meant what he said, but she wasn't sure. She also wasn't ready to take a chance on moving, not yet. She just didn't know what to do or think. Her mind slipped to prayer as she stared ahead, watching the grass and weeds and flowers blow in the light breeze, hearing the calls of the birds return once more as did the chatter of the animals and the sounds of the insects. She shuddered, knowing exactly what he had meant, that if no one found her and she could not move herself, the insects would find the stab wound.

Chapter 28

How much later it was, Fynn was never able to fully say. She had closed her eyes once more, her body still tense, her muscles aching from the strain of laying still. She heard the sounds of the grass moving from legs swishing through it and heard the silence that descended at the disturbance. She felt rather than heard someone drop to a knee beside her, a hand on her shoulder. She caught herself before she jumped in fright, her eyes opening and turning to stare at the man in uniform who knelt beside her.

"Dr. Daley?" Robert, the ERT leader, tilted his head to watch Fynn's reaction, seeing first relief and then fear. "Are you okay? Let's get you on your feet."

Fynn didn't dare shake her head, and her voice was very low as she spoke.

"No, I can't. I can't move."

"You can't move or you won't move."

She gave a small cry as Robert's hand reached to gently grasp her arm, ready to help her sit up. He paused at the look on her face, raising his eyes to his second-in-command who stood watching.

"I can't. I don't want to die." Fynn had forgotten momentarily that she was a professional in her career, well thought of in that, and became just a frightened young woman, afraid of what might happen if she did move.

Robert's voice was calming as he spoke. "Is there a particular reason that you can't?"

Fynn gave a small sigh, hardly daring to breath in case she moved when she shouldn't. The man had cut her bonds and she had one arm tucked her her head, the other hand flat on the ground beside her.

"I can't. If I move, I'm dead." Her eyes shifted to watch the other four ERT members surround them, backs to her, their eyes searching for her assailant. "He made me lie like this. He said I was laying on something, that if I moved, a needle would inject me and I would die."

Robert's hand rested gently on her shoulder as he stared at her, not quite sure he had heard her correctly. He raised his eyes once more to Patrick, who was staring at Fynn, shock on his face.

"Patrick, send someone to find the bomb squad. I want Theodore here. He'll have an idea of what we can do." His head turned as he heard a voice. "Alice? What did you say?"

"I said, when we found her, that's what she said. That's why you were asked to come in and also Theodore and his squad." She looked behind him. "There's Theodore now."

"Fynn? I'll be right back. I just need to speak Theodore. He's our bomb squad leader. I think he'll have an idea on how to get you back on your feet again."

Robert rose, approaching Theodore, a tall lanky man dressed in his gear.

"Robert? What do we have?"

"Dr. Daley was kidnapped earlier and brought here. She states she is laying on something, that if she moves, a needle will inject her with a deadly dose of a drug."

Theodore shook his head. "That's a new one. What do you need from us?"

"First, I need you to take a look and see what you can find."

Theodore nodded before he turned, sending one of his team running for their rig, to bring the shovel he decided they needed.

"We can dig down around her and see what we can find. I'll need your men to help stabilize her if we have to take out too much dirt." He pointed to the other side of Fynn. "Right there, Stuart. You have the shovel. Dig carefully around on the other side. We're looking for a box or something that is underneath her." Theodore paced around Fynn, his eyes assessing the ground under her. He finally pointed to an area near her back and hip. "I would suspect right there. The ground seems to have been disturbed."

The officer dug carefully, his eyes on Fynn at times, before his shovel hit a metal object. He stopped, drawing in a deep breath, waiting for Theodore to approach. Bending down, his hands reaching to dig away the dirt, Theodore paused for a moment, his eyes on the box before he looked at Fynn.

"Dr. Daley? Exactly what did he tell you?"

She sighed, her eyes drifting closed as she thought back, trying to focus, but having difficulty doing just that. "He said I was on a box. If I move, it would make a lid slid back or something like that and then I would be injected with a lethal amount of drug. He didn't say what drug." She frowned, before her eyes turned up to Robert. "That didn't make sense. Usually they tell you what drug it is."

"Not all the time." Robert's hand gripped her shoulder gently. "Theodore?"

Robert stood and moved away with Theodore, who had sent one of the men back to their rig to retrieve a thin metal plate.

"We need to slid the plate under her before we move her. It will be tricky. I can't assess like I want to. I don't want to dig down too much further in case it shifts."

Robert nodded, his eyes on the ground around Fynn. "If I can raise her body just a fraction of an inch, you may be able to slide it under her. When that happens, I'll grab her and run." He studied the plate Theodore had been handed. "Good. It's long enough that once we feed it under her, we can have one of our men on each end."

"That's my thoughts. Okay, let's do this. I have no idea how long she's been out here but she needs to be seen." Theodore looked up as Alice approached. "Alice?"

Alice shook her head. "It's the paramedic team. It's Brady and his partner."

"And that is a problem how?" Robert had a suspicion of why, but he needed to know for sure.

"Brady and Dr. Daley are a couple, How close, I'm not sure. I know others from the Foundation are down there, waiting."

"Then, let's go, Theodore." Robert walked back to crouch beside Fynn, assessing her and seeing the fear and stress on her face.

Chapter 29

Fynn watched as Robert dropped down near her, wanting to know what his plans were but afraid that it would mean she would be hurt. Lord, please? Let Brady know how much I love him, please? I know I needed to come here, I needed to heal, but it doesn't seem as if I'm going to even get that chance.

"Fynn?" Robert's hand rested gently on her arm. "Here's our plan. Theodore has that metal plate that we're going to slide under you. He has the box unburied on one side. I'll lift you just a bit to let him work it under you. We need you to trust me, to let me move you. We don't want you moving on your own. Just relax and let us do all the work."

She frowned at him before grumbling. "That's easy for you to say. You're not the one laying here on a box, just waiting to be stuck with a needle and die."

Robert grinned for a moment and then nodded at Theodore. Moving carefully and in tandem, Theodore and Robert worked away to slid the metal plate underneath Fynn. Robert felt her tensing as his arms slid under her back and knees, but she closed her eyes and resolutely remained as still as she could. Finally, Theodore nodded at him.

Robert waited for a moment, knowing that if they had guessed wrong, it could be Fynn who paid for their mistake. He took a deep breath, his eyes back on Fynn before he quickly moved, pulling her up and away from the ground, hands on the back of his vest to pull him up and back. He stumbled for a moment as the same hands helped to steady him on his feet, his eyes on Fynn. He realized that her body had gone limp and decided that was no surprise. He turned, heading for the road and to the paramedics, the others on his team surrounding them, Alice keeping step with him.

Will approached as he saw Robert and his burden, fear in his heart before Robert looked up.

"She's fainted, Will. I doubt that's like her, but given what she just went through, it's normal."

"The weapon, and it is a weapon?"

"Theodore and his squad are looking after it. He'll want the techs to move in before he takes it away. So far, we have it stabilized under a metal plate." Theodore looked towards the paramedics. "I hear Brady's here?"

"He is. I'm not happy about that, but he was the one who took the call."

"The luck of the draw." Robert shot a glance behind him. "I think you'll want to take a look at whatever it is that Theodore has found." He walked away, leaving Will staring after him before he walked back the way Robert had just come.

Brady stood, his heart in his mouth, watching as Robert approached. He didn't like it that his lady had been kidnapped again. He didn't understand why she was out here or why Robert was carrying her.

Brady reached for his stethoscope, watching closely as Robert placed Fynn on the stretcher, tucking her hands close to her body.

"She's had a knife wound, Brady. I'm not sure how long it has been, but she was laying with that side down in the dirt." Robert watched as Brady looked up in shock before he nodded. "Deliberate, Brady. We weren't supposed to find her. Not yet."

Brady nodded before he turned to confer with his partner, Fred, who nodded even as he reached to start an IV and then carefully cut away Fynn's T-shirt to reveal the wound. All three men drew in a breath at the look of it.

Finally lifting the stretcher into the rig, Brady slid in beside her, Robert following.

"I'm not leaving her, Brady. I promised to get her safe. I want to make sure that happens."

Brady walked behind the stretcher into the Emergency Department, his eyes finding Doc heading his way. Thank you, Lord. Doc's here. Just the one we need. Fynn is going to just disappear on me, if this keeps happening, and I would lose part of me. I want to marry her so quickly, but she needs this time. I just ask that she gets a chance to enjoy life without any more difficulty, but somehow, Lord, I don't see that happening.

"Brady? It's Fynn?"

"It is, Doc. Long story short, she was left with the wound in the dirt. I haven't heard all the circumstances surrounding it, but from what Robert said, she was afraid to move. He didn't say why."

Doc nodded, pointing to one of the exam rooms, a nurse following closely. "Give me your report, and then head out. If you weren't on duty, I would let you stay."

Brady nodded, devastation flickering across his face as he and Fred wheeled the stretcher into the room and then carefully lifted Fynn to the bed. His report given, he stood for a moment, his hand on Fynn's face before he moved away, Fred hesitating as he watched him.

"Talk to Robert, Doc. There's more than what we were told. It was a few hours she was like that from what I gather."

Doc shot him a keen glance, before he looked past him and frowned. Why was that man back here, he wondered, before he nodded to a security guard to approach him. The man was gone but not before shooting a look of hatred at Fynn.

Fred caught up with Brady as he stood near their rig, eyes on the horizon.

"Brady?"

"Yeah?" Brady shook his head, his own eyes finding the man now watching him. He pulled out his phone on a pretext and snapped a photo of him, sending it onto to both Dallas and Eric. "Sorry, Fred. Not a good day."

"It's been a bad day all around. Listen, I talked to Sam. He's made arrangements for Colin to come in early and take the rest of your shift."

"He has? That's great." Brady walked around the rig and stood before a moment before he opened the door and slid in. "Heading back to headquarters, are we?"

"We are. I'm sorry about your lady."

"Thanks." Brady stared out of the side window, his eyes not on the passing scenery as his thoughts shifted to Fynn. "I want whoever it was."

"We all do, Brady. For your sake and for hers." Fred shot him a glance, before he shook his head. "Doc will take good care of her."

"I know, but it hurts to see her hurting."

Chapter 30

Fynn's eyes flickered open and she frowned as she glanced around before she sighed. The hospital. That's right, she thought. Here I am, back in the hospital and I have no idea why or how or even who did it. She tried to roll to her side and stopped as a swift shaft of pain stopped her. Now, what did I do? I must have been pretty clumsy, she thought. God, are You there? Do You even care that I am hurt? I guess in my head I know that You do. It's the heart that's having trouble understanding that. Guess that's where my trust comes in. She didn't have her phone, she realized, not knowing where it was.

Footsteps approached her bed and then stopped. She heard soft breathing and muttered words before a hand reached to smooth her hair. She leaned into it before she looked up.

"Brady? What are you doing here? Aren't you working?" She frowned again, seeing that he wasn't in his uniform. "You were working today. What time is it?"

"Just after four. Sam had someone come in and cover for me. He somehow decided that I needed to be with you."

"And why would he think that?" Fynn sounded grumpy, she knew, and then spoke quietly. "I'm sorry. I'm not great company right now."

"Not a problem." Brady leaned his arms on the bed rail, his hands clasped as he studied them. "Fynn? We need to talk."

"About what? I don't remember what happened, other than I was laying on the ground and someone in a monster suit found me and then brought in a whole bunch more men in monster suits." Robert and Theodore were standing behind Brady, grins on their faces at her grumbling.

"And glad we are that you are safe." Robert moved to the end of the bed. "How are you now, Fynn?"

"Grateful to you and Theodore, is it? I don't remember leaving there."

"You fainted." Robert laughed at the disbelieving look on her face. "You really did. Doc says it was expected, that your body had to relax once you were out of danger. No problem, Fynn. We won't stay for long. We just wanted to ensure you were safe and on the mend."

"Safe? Now, that's an interesting word to use." Fynn shared a look with Brady. "I don't think that I'm all that safe, not yet. Dallas was by and said they hadn't found the man, but that he had been seen here. Know anything about that, Brady?"

Brady shook his head even as he grinned. "You caught me. I found the man watching me, snapped a quick photo and sent it on to Dallas and, yes, even on to Eric."

"Great! Now, Eric will be locking me away somewhere and throwing away the key." Fynn knew she was out of sorts but felt that she had every right to be, before she shook her head. "I'm sorry. That was uncalled for. Please, forgive me?"

"No apologies needed. Eric won't do that. He'll leave that up to me." Brady's grin widened as her eyes narrowed and she glared at him.

Fynn waved as Robert and Theodore left, knowing that she had to talk to Brady, but how did she do that? She loved him with all her heart but she felt she was bringing danger closer to him every day.

"Before you say a word, I'm not leaving." Brady shook his head. "Not one inch. You mean to much to me, Fynn darlin'."

"What have they told you, Brady? He grabbed me at the library, shoved me into the trunk of his car, and then drove around before he forced me to walk to that clearing and then shoved me down. He wanted me to die. I wasn't to be found, you know. He told me that the insects would find me before anyone else."

"You can thank Bradon for the quick find. He was looking for you, found your car at the library and then Dallas found him. Long story short? They were able to find the vehicle, which was from out of province and stolen, and then find you. I wasn't supposed to take that call. Will had asked that I not, but God knew I needed to be there."

Fynn's face softened. "He did. The verse that I kept hearing was "I am the God that heals you". Is that what God is doing in all this?" Her head went back. "One of Abe's men has a saying that we don't know the plans and purposes God has for us. That is just too true."

"It is." Brady snagged a chair with his toe and pulled it over, slumping down in it, fatigue running through him. "Doc said you could go home tonight."

"I can?" Fynn looked around. "Brady, where can I go where they won't find me? They're getting bold. I am afraid that your friends or the ladies will get hurt."

Brady watched her for a moment, his thoughts tumbling over one another. "They know the risk. It's what we do, Fynn. We have each other's backs. That's a given. Now that you're part of our family, they will watch for you as well." Brady gave a groan.

"Brady?"

He shook his head, a slight smile on his face. "It's just that we never talked about something. When the guys marry, their wives automatically became employees of the Foundation and receive a salary." He held up a hand at her protest. "It's how Barnabas and his father and then the board wanted to do it. That frees the ladies up to work the same way we guys do, or volunteer, or even go back to school. It is not mandated that they have to work. The board is fine with that."

"Wow! I don't think I've ever heard of that before." Fynn sat up, swinging her legs off the side of the bed, pulling the scrub top that she had been given to wear into a more comfortable position. "How come?"

"How come?" Brady shrugged. "Each one of us questioned Barnabas when we came on board and he said that the way they felt about it was that they wanted to encourage the couples, not make it more difficult for them. Expanding the options available for the couples makes it easer in some ways and more difficult."

She finally nodded. "That sounds like something Paul would have suggested, I think. He had a great encourager for himself in Barnabas." Her voice died away as her head tilted so she could look up at the ceiling, her hands clasping in her lap. "He's a wonderful man. I want to meet his parents."

"They've been around but I don't think that it's been when you have. We're to have the monthly potluck this Sunday and I heard that they would be there." Brady's voice stopped as he watched Fynn, having heard the door open and close behind him. When no one approached them, Brady started to turn, stopping as he felt the muzzle of a revolver on his neck. His eyes were on Fynn as she paled even more and he could see the shadows of fear in her eyes.

Chapter 31

Fynn froze as she saw the man. It was him, once more, she thought. I thought he had disappeared. Lord, now what? Where will we end up? I know it won't be good, wherever it is.

"So, little lady, you didn't die after all. Such a shame! You've made it difficult for me, you know." The man's hoarse voice sounded loud in the room. "Here's what we are going to do. You and your boyfriend here are going to walk out of here, right ahead of me. No tricks, young man, or she dies. And the same for you, little lady." He motioned with his revolver.

Fynn's eyes turned to Brady, who gave a slight shake of his head. They had not choice, he thought, and Lord, we need You to step in somehow. He rose, his hand reaching for Fynn's, leading her from her hospital room and then down the stairs, hitting the panic bar on the steel door at the bottom of the stairs and walking out into the darkness. A hand shoved him forward as Fynn gave a small scream, quickly subdued as a man appeared in front of them, a weapon in his hand as well.

"To the van. Move it!"

They were shoved forward and then into the van, Fynn's hand tight in Brady's again, as blindfolds were wrapped around their heads and then Fynn's hand was torn from Brady's and rough rope was wound around her wrists and pulled tight. She bit back a whimper. She had more backbone than this, she thought. She could feel Brady's arm agains hers and wanted so much to feel it around her, to feel his protection, but knew that would not happen. Not yet.

Brady felt the van shift as it left the hospital grounds, not stopping at the barrier, the wood breaking as it was hit at a high rate of speed. He could hear yells from the security guards. Please, Lord, let them find us quickly. I fear for Fynn.

He tried to follow the twists and turns of the speeding van, but was unable to. He sighed to himself, trying to come up with a plan but unable to. He was determined to protect his lady, no matter what happened.

Thirty minutes later, Branigan and Burnie stood in Fynn's hospital room, surprise on their faces at not finding either one. They turned as they heard footsteps and the nurse appeared, paperwork in her hand.

"Why? Where is Dr. Daley?" She looked around, not seeing her or Brady. "Brady was here with her. She didn't leave, did she?"

"Brady would not have let her go without that." Branigan pointed to the paperwork. "He's a stickler for that, you know." He looked around before heading for the door and then the stairs, looking for a security guard. A quick word with one and he was following the guard to their control room, watching as the video stream for the past hour outside of Fynn's door was pulled up.

"There. Who's that?"

The guard took a look. "You know, he's been hanging around here today. One of our guys approached him and he took off almost on a run. We reported it. You don't think he's responsible?"

"Given what happened earlier to Fynn, I would say it's a good chance that he is." Branigan paused, lost in thought. "Can we pull up any from outside the building? I would think the back, where there is less traffic." He watched again. "There. Brady and Fynn. They're not going on their own. What! The van drove right through the barrier. We'll never catch them."

"We didn't know. I'm sorry. We thought it was someone who didn't want to pay for parking." The guard was contrite.

"Not your fault. You didn't know." He paused again, before turning to leave. "Dallas from the police will be speaking with you all. We need to find them. This is the second time today Fynn has been kidnapped."

The guard spun in his chair, mouth open, as he stared at Branigan in shock, unable to say anything.

Burnie met Branigan at the bottom of the stairs, his eyes watching his friend closely.

"Branigan?"

"Yeah?" Branigan finally looked up, a frown on his face. "Sorry. She's been kidnapped again, along with Brady. There were two. One forced them outside where another one was waiting. The guard says it was likely the van they were in that tore through the barriers at the gate. That was reported, but I'm not sure if they got a plate number or not."

"That's not good." Burnie spun, almost running down the hallway. "We need to find the rest of the guys. We have a lot of work to do."

"That we do." Branigan pulled his phone out as it chimed. "Emma's sent something." He tossed his keys to Burnie. "You drive. I want to see what Emma has to say. If she's up at this hour working, it must be important."

"Fynn says she's like that. If it involves a friend or a child, she won't sleep until Abe makes her or their son needs her."

Chapter 32

Barnabas watched the men as they mingled in the conference room, shock on their faces and in their voices. They spoke quietly before they found seats, pulling up programs on the computers, reaching for pen and paper, brainstorming.

Breck stood beside him before he moved away, heading for where Branigan stood, his eyes on the wall, not moving. His phone was in his hand as he thought through the information that Emma had forwarded on to him. I have no idea how she has found this. Fynn's brother has been here. That must have been who Brady spoke to on the way back from the lake. He never did tell us, did he? Lord, please? Protect them. Put a hedge around them. Bring them back safely to us. I know they are making plans, I am just not sure what they are

"Branigan?" Breck's voice broke into his revert and he jumped slightly, meeting Breck's quick grin as he turned. "Sorry. I didn't mean to startle you. You were deep in thought?"

"I was. Emma sent some interesting information to me. We need to look at it. I've sent it to the printer, enough copies for us all and Will and Dallas. I suspect Eric will want copies as well."

"Has anyone spoken to Eric?"

"I think Burnie was going to." He turned, searching the room for Burnie. "Eric's here. I didn't see him arrive."

Breck gave another grin. "I think we should just offer him an apartment here. He's here enough." He paused, a thought rising. "Does Eric remember Fynn's brother?"

Branigan shrugged as he heard a voice from beside him and turned to find Dallas standing there.

"I asked him that very question. They're around the same age. He says he does to a certain extent but he was only five when the brother disappeared. He has heard his mother and father speak of him. But that was too many years ago for Eric to be certain what are his memories and what are theirs." He looked up as he heard Buckley's voice.

Buckley had risen from his chair, his eyes on Barnabas before he looked around.

"Let's pray, my friends. Like we normally do. We have one extra, no, Doc's here. We can break up into twos. Brady and his lady need our prayers. We have no idea where they are or if they've been hurt. God needs to be in control."

"God is in control, Buckley. We just don't see it." Doc nodded at Dallas. "You're with me, Dallas. Let's find some seats."

Thirty minutes later, they all shifted in their chairs, looking up in surprise as the four younger ladies, Berneen's brother, Darby, and Anna entered, trays of food in their hands. This is needed, Brendon thought. Thank you, Lord, for these ladies. Now, open our eyes. Help us to find our friends.

Barnabas turned away, his emotions overcoming him for a moment. He had grown to appreciate Fynn's understated sense of humour, as morbid and dark as it was at times. She had laughed at him once when he had commented on that, just saying that when you worked in a medical field, you used black humour sometimes to cope. He could appreciate that. He walked away, his phone in his head. He just needed to speak with his father, to hear his thoughts and then his prayers, to hear the verses his mother would draw from her memory for him. They were away right now, and he knew that. It still didn't stop him from wanting to talk to them.

He returned to find the group staring at Burnie, who stood, his hand up, distress on his face.

"Burnie?"

Burnie spun as he heard Barnabas' voice and then walked rapidly towards him, pointing out the door.

"Burnie?"

"I just caught a call from Will. He's on his way to the bluffs. Someone reported a van going over them." Burnie could barely get the words out.

Barnabas froze, his hand half raised to rub at his face before he dropped it. "Where?"

"The bluffs. Near our end, he said."

Barnabas spun. "Come with me, Burnie. We can be spared. Let's head that way and see what Will can tell us."

Behind the wheel of his vehicle, Barnabas paused before he shoved the gear stick into drive and took off, a little faster than his normal speed. "What have we discovered so far?"

"Not much on our part. Emma's sent through a lot on both Eric and Fynn's brother. They called him Flannery but that wasn't his name. Eric couldn't explain why he was called that. His legal name is Farr."

Barnabas shot him a look, before he pulled to a stop behind Will's police vehicle, shoving the transmission into park. "I have met a Farr. A few years ago. He works in town here, as a paralegal." He sighed, a hand rubbing at his chin. "That's who she looks like."

"Say what?" Burnie studied his friend.

"Fynn. She looks like Farr. I never made the connection, just wondered who it was." He shoved open his door, his attention moving to Will, who stood watching them. "Will?"

"Barnabas. Burnie. I didn't expect you to be here, but I should have. Any word?"

Barnabas shook his head. "None, but we know who her brother is."

"You do? Who?" Will turned as he heard the heavy sound of a Diesel engine and moved to one side for the tow truck to approach. "I'm praying, guys, but it's tough. I thought I told your men that I didn't want any more adventures like the four had."

Barnabas shook his head. "I told them that, too. Brennen's response was that if only four had adventures, that left the rest of us not finding our ladies."

Will laughed. "So, he's saying that in order to find your ladies, you have adventures. Not like Bradon's, please. It was too close a call for him."

Barnabas' attention shifted to the activity near the edge of the bluffs. "What can you tell us, Will?"

"Not a lot yet. It was empty, but it looks as if it was deliberately sent over. The team will take at quick look here and then go over it with a fine tooth comb once they get it back to the yard. It does match the description of the van from the hospital." Will excused himself as he heard his name called.

"Alice?" He stood for a moment, peering over the edge at the activity below him.

"They're not there. From the looks of it, it was left in drive and then shoved forward. We've found footprints."

Will nodded, his eyes rising to meet Barnabas'. "Keep me informed. I'll be at the Foundation Building."

"Of course. The techs should have a preliminary report shortly."

Chapter 33

Three days had passed, with no sign of the two. Will had been around, his keen eyes on their friends, but not saying much of what he knew. Dallas had been called away due to the sudden illness of a close relative but was due back the next day. Barnabas had been putting out feelers, but not getting any response, which both surprised and perplexed him. He had confided in Breck that must mean the two were not in town.

The men had all taken leave from their work to dedicate their time to their research, but even at that, they were not finding out too much. Branigan had gone on a search, accompanied by Burnie, looking for Farr. A source had told him that Fynn's brother was still around but had taken to hiding and wearing a disguise. Breck had sighed. That meant he knew he was being sought and not by Fynn.

Berneen had taken Cadee with her and gone on a search through town, almost to every home and business. Darby had sought out his friends and searched in the surrounding woods and parks and down by the beach. He had even been seen at the marina, checking out any boats that might be hiding the two.

Buckley had spent his time divided, part with his friends, the other part with his congregants, leading in the hourly prayer groups that were set up. Everyone was on a search, but no one had found them. Nor heard a word.

Brody and Brandon had taken Doc with them that day, heading for a larger centre, hoping that they could find someone who had seen them. Brenden was deep in research, Eric helping as he could. They were all puzzled that not a sign of the two had been found. There had been no communication from their kidnappers.

Barnabas turned from his computer, rubbing at his eyes. He was disheartened, he thought, and then took that burden to the Lord. Lord, where are they? We're looking but not finding them. And that I don't understand. Please, Lord? Where do we search? He rose and walked towards the large map Darby had taped to the wall, marking off where they had searched. His finger traced along the shoreline, stopping at the spot where the van had been dumped. Barnabas frowned. Now, what was it about the particular area of the bluffs that bothered him?

Ennis watched for a moment, Bradon beside her, before she walked over, her head tilting as she ran her finger along the map, much like Barnabas had just done. Her finger stopped, and she tapped at a spot.

"There's an abandoned farm right here, Barnabas. Do you remember? I know we used to go there, as teens, just to look around. The guys used to try and scare us with ghost stories."

Barnabas' body stilled before he nodded. "It's close to where they dumped the van. I don't want to say anything to Will. Come on, you two. Let's go take a look." He turned and almost on a run, headed for his vehicle, Ennis and Bradon right behind him.

Barnabas stopped his vehicle at the end of the overgrown lane and ducked his head to see through the windshield, his fingers tapping on the steering wheel.

"Someone's been through here."

Bradon leaned forward, an arm resting on the seat back, as he too scoured the area for any signs of the culprits.

"And recently too. More than once, I would say."

Ennis nodded. "There's a second entrance that not many people know of. Not unless they know the property."

Barnabas snapped his fingers. "You're right. I had forgotten."

Quickly backing up, he drove away and then turned onto a gravel road. He could tell it had not been travelled much, at least not in the last couple of days. He pulled off the road and then shifted to look at Ennis and then Bradon.

"Well? Do we go in?"

Ennis nodded and reached for the door handle, Bradon's hand coming to rest on her shoulder.

"We need to pray and pray hard. I have this feeling that we need to find them today and now."

"You and me, both." Barnabas prayed and then slid from his vehicle, Ennis and Bradon following suite.

Ennis took the lead, walking rapidly, her hands reaching to push branches, weeds, and long grass from her path. Coming to a stop, she studied the buildings. The barn, she noted, had collapsed almost totally. Not surprising, she thought.

Bradon gave a low whistle. "Wow! You said it was abandoned. I certainly didn't expect to see this."

Barnabas shook his head. "It's been a few years since I was out here. Let's head for the house."

Ennis shook her head. "No. That would be too obvious." She tapped her mouth with a long forefinger, the pale peach nail polish reflecting the sun. "There's a root cellar and a storm cellar. Between the house and the barn." She went to move forward but a sudden noise stopped her in her tracks and then the three stepped backwards into shelter, watching as a ramshackle truck that was more rust than blue drove in and a man jumped down, grabbing a plastic shopping bag and heading for the house. They waited, not able to see if he had entered the house or not. An hour later, he returned to his truck and drove away.

Ennis looked around and then ran quickly for the house, heading for the back, the two men on her heels before Bradon's hand stopped her

"Let one of us go ahead, Ennis. I don't want to answer to your parents or brother if something happens to you."

She nodded, impatient to be searching. Barnabas studied the building before he spoke in a low voice.

"Where are the cellars?"

She pointed. "The root cellar is there. The storm cellar is closer to the barn."

The men nodded before moving out, Ennis' hand on Bradon's back.

They paused as they reached the root cellar, seeing the shiny new hasp on it, and the open padlock. Glances were exchanged before Bradon reached for the lock, removed in and then shoved the door open. Barnabas entered, climbing down the rickety few wooden steps, brushing away the cobwebs, his eyes searching. He could see debris left over from years ago. The musty, mouldy smell hit him as did the dust he had stirred up. Shadows briefly blocked the sun before he turned and climbed back out.

"It's been disturbed, but I can't tell if it was Brady or Fynn or just some animal." He looked around as he brushed at his hair. "The storm cellar?"

"This way." Ennis headed towards the barn, almost on a run and then detoured to her left, stopping short of the cellar, hidden for a moment by the overgrown brush. "It's here." She glanced around, nervous, feeling as if she was being watched. "Someone's out here."

"I feel it, too." Bradon brushed by her, heading for the door, pausing as he saw, once more, the hasp and this time a closed padlock. "There's a lock here. Someone wants either to keep people out or keep people in."

"I would say to keep them in." Barnabas looked around. "We need to break it open. The wood is likely rotten, but it seems to have been repaired to some extent."

Bradon agreed, looking around for a long rock, stopping short at the metal pipe waving near his face. He gave a quick grin at the smirk Ennis threw him. "Thank you, love."

"Where did you find that?" Barnabas studied it before he turned to her.

"Right there. I have no idea why it's there, but it's not rusted."

"No, you're right. It's not." Bradon paused. "Barnabas, pray please. I think we've found them, but I'm afraid of the condition that we'll find them in."

"I know. I keep thinking of how close it was to losing you two."

Once more, Bradon reached for the lock, this time prying at it with the metal bar. A snap and the hasp separated from the door and the door opened slightly. The three paused, staring at each other, hesitant to move forward but knowing they needed to.

Chapter 34

A tap at his door had Will raising his head from his paperwork, a sigh stifled quickly as he saw Alice standing there, hesitant it seemed to disturb him, her glance shifting between his office and back down the hallway.

"Alice? Is there something you wanted?"

Her head whipped around as Will spoke and she nodded. "There is. There's a man here who wants to speak with you."

"There is?" When she didn't continue, he rose and walked towards her. "And does this man have a name?"

She nodded. "Farr McIntosh."

"Farr McIntosh?" Will puzzled at the name before his brow cleared. "Farr, is it? And I would gather he is here about Fynn."

"I think so. Where would you like me to put him for you?"

Will raised a hand. "Let me get a glimpse of him first. Then, we'll see." Will followed Alice back down the hall, standing just out of sight of the front desk and reception, his eyes on the man standing with his back towards him, watching out the window. *He's nervous, and I wonder why.* "Bring him back to my office. Give me five minutes. I want to grab a coffee and I'm sure he could use a coffee or tea. Ask him as you bring him back. I want you nearby."

"Sure, Will."

Will sat back at his desk, his coffee mug nearby, as he stared down at the budget he was to be working on. He sighed. It would have to wait, he thought. Fynn and Brady came first. He looked up as Alice tapped at his door and then stood, assessing the younger man who stood, hesitant, shifting slightly from foot to foot as he watched Will.

"Farr McIntosh?" At the man's nod, Will pointed to a chair. "Alice got you a coffee?"

Farr nodded, his eyes dropping to the mug he held, his hand shaking slightly before he reached to set the mug on the table beside his chair. He looked up, and Will saw the resemblance to Fynn, although his hair was a deeper red than Fynn's copper locks and his eyes a dark enough brown to be almost black.

Will sat in the chair beside him, his own mug in his hand, and waited, knowing that Farr was there for a reason. He had time, he thought, to wait.

"Chief Peters?" Farr finally looked around, settling back in his chair. "I understand you know Fynn Daley?"

"I do. She's dating a young friend of mine. Why?"

Farr sighed. "This is so hard." His face became buried in his hands. "I have no idea where to start."

"The beginning is usually a good spot." Will grinned as Farr's head shot up and he stared at him dumbfounded. "Take your time."

Farr nodded. "It usually is, but I can't start at the very beginning. I am only just remembering things. One of those things is that I have a sister. A sister named Farr. And she is in great danger."

Will nodded. "I understand. Tell me your story."

Farr's eyes grew distant as he began to tell his story, a story that Will had already partly determined.

"I am sure you are aware from Fynn that I disappeared from my parents when I was about six. Maybe Eric, I am beginning to remember him as well, would have said something. I didn't remember them. Honest." He looked up at Will, tears in his eyes for a moment. "I have no idea why I was taken or why I was kept from them. The couple who took me drove that memory down inside me. They were abusive at first and then began to ignore me. I had what I needed to survive and nothing more. I found a church when I was a teenager and became involved, eventually realizing I was a sinner and accepting Christ's sacrifice for me. I know I need to heal, but I am not sure how.

"Anyway, the couple are involved in white collar crime. I would hear them talking sometimes when they didn't think I was around. I finally began to write everything down. That notebook is in a safety deposit box in town. They are from this town. I will tell you their names but I need to get through this first.

"McIntosh is not the name I was raised under. I was never adopted. They told me I wasn't worth the time or money to do that. I still don't understand, but they seemed to have something on my biological father or mother, which one I am not sure."

"We can sort it out. But what brings you here today?" Will was watchful, his mind racing at the possibilities of who it could be before he nodded. He had a good idea who the couple was. In fact, he was sure he had seen Farr with them around town over the years. "Go on."

"I had to come forward. A few weeks ago, I heard them talking about a Dr. Daley. That they had sent a man to find her and kill her for some reason. That reason, I don't know. They never came out and said." He looked up, tears momentarily blinding him. "I need to save her, Chief Peters, but I don't know how. I've tried to find her the last couple of days but haven't been able to. I did speak with the man that I have seen her with, but he didn't say anything. Do you know where she is?"

Will sat back, knowing he would have to put Farr somewhere he would be safe, but not quite sure if he was on the up and up.

"She's missing, Farr. She and Brady disappeared about three days ago."

"Oh, no! They have them!" Farr shot to his feet, agitation in his body, and began to pace. "Where would they put them?"

"That's what we are working on. I want you to talk to the detective, Dallas, who is in charge of the case but first, we need to put you somewhere." Will stood, reaching for his keys and pointing to the door. "We'll go out back. The Foundation Building is the best spot for now"

"I can't go there!" Farr stopped dead in his tracks, horror mingled with hope on his face. "They'll blame me."

"To the contrary, no. All of us have been trying to find you. They want that for Fynn."

"You have? They do?" Hope sprung to his eyes. "What can I do to help find her?"

"Right now, the best thing is to come with me and then stay in the building. There's security there. Breck will set you up in a suite."

"Thank you, Chief. I don't know what to say."

"It's Will. It looks as if we are going to be friends." Will grew stern. "And if this is a ploy to harm either one of them, you'll answer to many men."

"It's not, Chief, I mean, Will. It's not. I lost so many years with my sister."

"And your sister with you." Will's hand raised to wave at the guard at the gate before he spoke again. "She only has just remembered having a brother. She buried it deep. I should give a bit of history. Your sister pushed her way through school, graduating at 20 as an entomologist. But like you, she didn't have the parental love and caring that she needed. She has found love and acceptance with all of us. I think she and Brady have come to terms and a wedding is in the offing. But we need to find them first."

A short while later, Will watched as Farr spoke with Doc and Anna, Breck at his side.

"You say he just walked in and asked for you?"

Will nodded. "He did. I'll fill you in on what I know, but there are some names I need Dallas to research."

Breck studied Farr for a moment. "I've seen him around town. I think I know who you mean." He grinned suddenly. "Let's see who finds out the information first. Say, did he ever change his name?"

"No, and that's part of the puzzle." Will looked around, seeing the intensity the men were working under. "Any word?"

"No. Barnabas, Bradon and Ennis took off a while ago. They had been looking at the map and then disappeared without saying where they were heading."

Will hesitated before he turned. "Keep me updated. I'm praying we find them." He glanced down at his phone. "Breck? The loading dock?"

Breck stared at him before he left the conference room on the run, waving at the security guard to follow, Will on his heels. They slid to a halt, watching as the door opened and Barnabas drove in, hearing the exhaust fans kick in to clear the air of fumes, before the overhead door slid down and Barnabas' vehicle door flew open.

Barnabas stood for a moment, watching inside the vehicle, before he turned, relief on his face as he nodded.

"We have them. We need the stretchers from the infirmary."

The security guard spun and left on a run, his hand on his mike to call for help.

Chapter 35

Barnabas stood for a moment, his eyes on Will, before he turned back to the vehicle, his hands reaching for Fynn and carrying her to the stretcher quickly wheeled towards him. He could hear muttered protests coming from Brady, and Bradon's laughter-filled voice commenting. Ennis walked beside Brady, a hand out to help balance him before he was swung up on the other stretcher. The three stood back, Breck and Will approaching them.

"Barnabas? You found them? How?" Will's voice was quiet before Barnabas nodded.

"Let me put my vehicle back outside." He turned, finding one of the security team beside him, hand stretched out for the keys. With a quiet word of thanks, he handed them over and then pointed towards the hallway. "Let's walk. Ennis, go find your ladies. We'll need to meet, but I think we'll need a meal first. Let's find out what Doc has to say."

Will paced beside Barnabas, Bradon keeping up with them, stopping as they came to the infirmary. Doc nodded as he brushed past them, Anna with him. He had used Brady's help in situations similar to this, not liking it that Brady was one of the ones he had to treat. He stopped by his stretcher, assessing him, letting Anna go on to Fynn's room. Anna was back in short order, her hand on Doc's arm, rushing him to Fynn.

The three men watched, concern on their faces, before Will turned to Barnabas.

"We need to talk."

Barnabas nodded. "We do. Let's head to my office. I want to talk to you first before I talk to the others. You'll need to send a team out to the old Miller farm."

"The Miller farm? Why? It's been abandoned for years. They can't sell it, it's in such bad shape."

"Exactly. That's where they were."

Will held up a finger, his phone out as he made the call. He was thoughtful as he pocketed it. "They'll head out that way. Alice is already making her way there. Something had been said to her that she felt she needed to investigate."

"Good." Barnabas sank down onto his couch, his eyes closing for a moment. Fatigue washed over him, the stress releasing. He jerked as he felt a hand on his shoulder and looked up, finding Breck standing beside him, a mug of coffee held out.

"Okay, my friend, talk."

Bradon's mind drifted back to the moment they had shoved the door open, Barnabas' voice fading as he spoke. The door had creaked open, dust mites and flies circling in the shafts of sunlight before they had stepped down, missing the broken steps as they did so. Their eyes were drawn to the rough shelving with debris on it. They could see the evidence of animals on them. An exclamation from Ennis drew their eyes downwards and they sprang forward, dropping to their knees, Bradon beside Brady, Barnabas beside Fynn. Their hearts were in their mouths as they reached for the wrists, their heads nodding at Ennis's question.

Bradon gently rolled Brady over, a groan coming from his friend. He heard Ennis' quickly indrawn breath at the bruises on his face.

"Brady? Can you hear me, buddy?" Bradon's voice, though low, sounded loud in the area.

"I can. I don't want to go to school today, Dad. Let me sleep. I'm sick." He tried to roll to his side, but a hand on his chest kept him on his back. "My chest hurts. I'm sick." He drifted off again, leaving Ennis and Bradon to exchange worried glances before Ennis moved to Fynn.

"Barnabas?"

"She's alive, Ennis, but sick. She's running a fever. I don't want to look at her wound. Not here. Not in this dirty place. Bradon?"

"Let's go. I don't like that we're here, not when someone could return shortly."

"I agree. Can you manage Brady?"

"Yeah, I think to. Help me get him up and outside and I'll swing him over my shoulder. Ennis? Stay back behind us until we're in the clear. I don't like having to walk across the yard."

Barnabas stood for a moment staring around the yard before he was back into the root cellar, gathering Fynn into his arms, her body limp, her head drooping over his arm until Ennis turned it into his shoulder.

"There's a path behind here that should lead us back to other side of the yard. I think I can find it."

"That's what I was trying to remember. Lead on, Ennis. I feel like we're running out of time."

"I think we are." She was off, finding the overgrown path and heading down it, watching carefully for the two men and their burdens. She opened the doors for the men and then slid in beside Fynn, her arm reaching to wrap around her friend.

"She's so hot, guys. Hurry!"

"I know she is. How's Brady?" Barnabas keyed the motor to life and drove off as quickly as he could.

"Still out of it. Who would do this?"

"That's what Dallas and Will are working on. Any word from our guys?"

Bradon pulled out his phone. "Brenden. He says they have found some information that they need to talk to us about. He's been trying to reach you."

"I felt my phone vibrate but we had other things to do. Anything else?" Silence greeted his question and his head turned for a moment, seeing the look of surprise on Bradon's face. "Bradon?"

Bradon shook his head as he felt Ennis' hand on his shoulder. "It's Breck. He said Will's at the building. And he has brought out Fynn's brother, Farr."

"Her brother?" Ennis's voice held surprise. "How did he find him?"

"It was the other way around, Breck said. Farr walked into the police department looking for Will."

"Good. They need each other. God has been in this so far. Both of them are alive. We'll catch up once we have these two safe." Barnabas pulled abruptly to the side of the road, his fingers tapping at the gearstick.

"Barnabas?" Ennis leaned past Bradon to search his face. "Why are you stopping?"

"I'm thinking. We can't take them to the hospital in town. Given their condition, their kidnappers will look for them there."

"Take them to Doc. He'll decide where they need to be. If he can treat them and have Anna stay with them, that may work." Ennis had full confidence in Doc and Anna. The older couple had become good friends of hers, almost as if they were a second set of parents, which they were to all of the younger people in the building.

"I agree." Bradon shifted to look into the back seat. "Fynn needs help. I don't like the fever she's running."

"Nor do I." Barnabas pulled away, finally drawing up in front of the building, his eyes searching around. "I feel like someone is out there, watching us."

"They are. Security has seen evidence of that even though they have not found anyone."

"I know." Barnabas sat, sorting through scenarios before he sighed. "I guess we'll have to take a chance."

"The loading dock." Ennis finally spoke up, stating what she felt was so obvious. "Go around to the loading dock, open the door, drive in, and close the door behind you. The windows on your vehicle are dark enough, and it's getting close enough to dusk, that they can't see in, whoever it is that's out there."

Bradon laughed at the expression of Barnabas' face even as his friend shook his head.

"Too obvious, wasn't it? I didn't even think of that. I was just trying to figure out how to get them from here to the door. Smart lady, you have there, Bradon."

Bradon grinned as he looked back at his wife. "She is. I keep telling her that. She just says it's God who telling her these things."

"Well, it is." Ennis sounded disgruntled. "Well? What are you waiting for? Sitting here doesn't get them to Doc and Anna."

The men laughed as Barnabas did exactly as she had requested, the door closing behind them, even as Bradon sent a text to Breck. They looked up to see the security guard, Will and Breck heading their way.

Chapter 36

Doc finally stood up, his eyes on Fynn, his hand reaching for her wrist. Her pulse was still threads, he thought, before he walked to the medication cabinet and unlocked it. He kept it stocked with what he felt he would need, and prayed that the antibiotics he would choose would work. Fynn had been upfront with him one day when they were talking, giving him her medical history, knowing that he wasn't asking just for curiosity. No allergies to medications. That was good, he said.

An hour later, he stood back, once more assessing her. He didn't like the high fever she was running but prayed that the cooling blanket and the antibiotics and pain medications would kick in. He had agreed with Will when the police chief had popped in. They didn't want to hospitalize her if they could help it. If Doc needed anything, Will had agreed to find it for him.

Anna stood for a moment, her eyes on her husband, before her arm was around him.

"Doc?

"I pray what I have done will work. Her wound looked good, all things considered."

"It did. When Bradon said where she was found, I was worried."

"You and me both." He turned. "Brady?"

"He's been awake and had some broth and water. He's sleeping. Naturally, I would say. It will take time for him to recover. Worrying about Fynn won't help."

"No, it won't. We'll need to get him in to see her for a few moments when we can." Doc paused, his eyes on his wife, praising God that He had given him such a helpmeet. "What's the story with those two?"

Anna smiled. "Brady let it slip that they are engaged. I gather from what he said she asked first and then he asked her. Buckley was there when Fynn asked."

"He was, and he wouldn't say a word, now would he?"

"Absolutely not. Barnabas was looking for you. He's hoping you can give an update on these two to everyone. Go. I'll send someone if I need you. And you need to call the centre. You're not going there today, I know that."

"No, I'm not. Thanks, love." Doc paused at the doorway, his eyes turning back to Fynn before he moved to stand in Brady's doorway. He sighed. *What is it with these young people, Lord? Can't they find love in the normal way, like Anna and I did? I know, You're in control. I just hate to see them hurt.* He turned to find Breck watching, waiting for him to walk towards him.

"Doc?"

"Brady's sleeping naturally, Anna says. We need to pray for Fynn. She's in rough shape. High fever. The wound seems fine but I have debrided it. I'll be watching it. They're waiting for me, Anna says."

Breck grinned. "They are, if you can spare the time. The ladies have brought in sandwiches and salads and fruit for us. They informed us we were working too hard and needed a break."

"They are right on both counts."

"I know, Doc. I know. But we want this over for Brady and Fynn."

"That we know. And we will. Just don't forget that God is leading in this. There is a reason for what they are going through. Fynn needs to heal from her past and so does her brother."

"Brady too. I don't know that he's ever really reconciled to his parents' deaths."

Doc's steps slowed before he nodded, having reached the conference room door. "I suspect you're correct, Breck. We all have things we need to heal from. That's where we come in for him. We need to encourage him to do just that. Fynn too. That's where the ladies come in. What they have been through will help. They all have a different perspective on life now. She needs to hear those."

"She has, Doc. I know she has. She told me she had and was working through what she was told and how she could apply those lessons to her life. She's hurting way deep inside. It will take time."

"That it will." Doc moved away, heading for the food and then sitting himself down at a table, his eyes watching his young friends as they mingled and then sat to eat. His gaze lingered on Barnabas for some reason, a prayer rising for the leader of these men. Something told him that in the not too distant future, Barnabas would be going through a fight for his own life and that frightened Doc.

Chapter 37

Will finally stood and walked away from the room, his phone out, turning to search the room to focus on Farr. He spoke quietly before he dialled another number.

"Dallas? Where are you right about now?"

At the urgency in Will's voice, Dallas stared at his phone for a moment before he answered. "Just getting up. I got in about nine this morning after driving all night. Why?"

"Because we have had a major turn in the investigation. Alice says she tried to reach you but got your voice mail. I'm at the Foundation. Fynn's brother walked into the detachment this morning, and I talked with him. Farr's here. It's a nasty piece of work that has been done."

"I can only imagine." Dallas swung his house door closed, checked it was locked and then ran for his car. "I''m on my way. I'm putting you on speaker."

"Good. Here's what we have. I haven't talked to the fellows here yet to find out what they have, but Alice said that someone called Tracker has been calling for you and then sending information by courier. Apparently you have a number of packages on your desk."

"Tracker? That's Emma. Didn't you know that?"

Will drew in his breath. "No, but I gather from what I've heard she keeps her identity hidden. It goes no further."

"No, sir. I'll stop by my office and grab what's there. I'll find a spot there to work."

"Good. Breck said he had a desk and computer set up that you could use, with its own printer. He anticipated that you would want to work here for a while before heading back into the office. For now, this has become part of our detachment, just so nothing can be said."

Dallas paused as he stepped into his office, a frown on his face. "That bad, Will?"

"That bad. The ones we are looking at have ties to the town council."

"Oh, great. Just what we needed." Dallas stared at his desk. "How much information did Emma send me?"

Will laughed. "That bad?" He hung up on Dallas' grumbling.

Barnabas walked towards him. "Will, we'll give you our statements if you like. Then, that's over with."

"Hold that thought. Dallas is on his way out. He'll take them."

"Sure, whatever." Barnabas didn't sound like himself. "There's something about that place that is bothering me."

"And that would be?"

Barnabas shrugged. "I'm not sure. Something different about it. I know it's been years since I've been out there as a teenager and I know it's decrepit, but something was off. I'll think of what it is at some point." He turned to stare back at the room. "What do you make of Farr?"

"Now, that's someone who is difficult to read. He's hiding something, but I can't pinpoint what it is."

"I know he is. I pray he doesn't hurt Fynn or Brady."

"No, I don't think he will. I think that he doesn't know us or trust us enough, given his history." Bradon stood beside them. "I've talked to him. He really didn't remember. The abuse he suffered drove it down so deep. It was when he heard the couple talking about a Dr. Fynn Daley that he began to research her and when he found her picture, the memories started to come back. Selective amnesia, maybe?"

"And the man Brady found is somehow connected to the couple. That's what Brennen and Baird are working on."

"Okay. What else do we need to do?"

"Find the Evans' family. They're involved. Their son was one of our kidnappers. I recognized his voice even though his face was covered." Brady stood beside them, shaky, but upright.

"Should you even be up, Brady?" Will's hand reached to steady him as concern flickered across the faces of the three men.

"I need to be. We need to solve this, find whoever it is. There is a deadline, guys. By Friday. They told me Fynn had to agree to something or find something by this Friday. If she didn't, she would die." He looked at them, distress and despair on his face. "I can't let them hurt her. I just can't."

"We won't, Brady. We're working hard on that. Emma's sending us information to help." Breck drew Brady into the room and to a seat, the room growing in silence as his friends stood and approached him, each with words of their own for him.

Brady looked around. "Where do we stand? And what can I do?"

"First, you give Dallas your statement. He's right here. Then, you talk to us. You tell us what you know. Hopefully we can get Fynn's side of the story."

Brady shook his head. "You won't. She won't tell it, not unless she has changed her mind. Whatever they said to her, it hurt her and drove her down. It broke her." Tears brimmed in his eyes and then overflowed, but he was not ashamed. His heart hurt too much for his lady. "She whispered to me that she had given up, that she just couldn't go on, not when she found out that someone at the lab was involved."

"That's what we thought. Did she say who?" Will had sat beside Brady, an arm leaning on the table.

Brady shook his head. "No, but she dropped enough hints that I think we can figure it out." His head dropped to his arms, causing the ones around him to exchange glances. "Where's Dallas? I want to give my statement, and then get in on the hunt." He stood as he heard a voice behind him.

Fynn sat there in a wheelchair, the only way Anna would let her up. Her face was pale, her hair a mess, and her eyes fever bright.

"Will? Can we talk? Can you take my statement?"

Will approached her, to crouch down in front of her. "I can do that. But you shouldn't be up."

"I have to be. Everyone here was threatened. I need to tell you who it is. And, God forgive me, I brought this to you." Her voice died away as she stared past Will. "Who? Is that? It can't be?" Her hand covered her trembling mouth as her emotions tried to overwhelm her. "Farr?"

"It is. But before you talk to him, you talk to me. I don't want anyone to come back on us to say the statements are contaminated and have the charges thrown out." Will reached for the handles on her chair, turning it and wheeling her away, following Breck as he headed for his office, knowing that Dallas and Brady were heading for Barnabas' office.

Chapter 38

Her head spinning as she sat upright, hardly able to keep her eyes open, Fynn struggled to find the words that she needed, to tell her story

"Okay, so. We were taken from the hospital. The man who forced us out is the man who left me in the field. I don't know how he knew where I was. He must have been watching. We were forced into a vehicle and then driven around for a long time. I lost track of the turns and stops, but I know we did go over railroad tracks many times. I think they were just driving around in circles. Or that's how it seemed."

Her mind traced back to that late afternoon into the evening. Brady had shown up in her hospital room, refusing to leave, just grinning at her as she tried to send him back to work. He was done work for the day, he informed her, Sam calling in someone to cover for him so he could be with his lady.

She frowned at him before she shook her head. "Is that what I am, Brady?"

"You are." He stood for a moment before he carefully gathered her close. "You're the one I've been waiting for. I thought I made that clear."

She sighed, her head on his shoulder, feeling his strength yet gentleness in how he held her. "You did. It's just that I've never had this before. Had someone tell me that they love me and really mean it."

Brady's heart broke for her. At that point, he was ready to sweep her out of the hospital room, find Buckley and a license and marry her right then and there. They spoke quietly for a while before her eyes looked past him. He saw the fear on her face and how it paled. Before he could turn, he felt the revolver pressed against him. No amount of protesting stopped the man from forcing them from the room and down the stairs, no staff or visitors in the hallway to see them or stop them.

Fynn stifled a scream as she saw the second man approaching them, his face covered with a bandanna and his sweatshirt hood pulled up over his face as far as as it could be. Forced into a van, she had clung to Brady's hand until she was forced to drop it and her wrists bound and a blindfold slapped ruthlessly around her head. She so wanted Brady's arm around her, not just touching her, but knew that wouldn't happen. She felt his arm moving and then his hands were gripping hers, stilling the trembling of hers with his strength.

After who knew how long, the van picked up speed and she twisted her head, listening. They had headed out of town for a while before the van slowed and then she felt the roughness of the ride pick up. A gravel road, she thought, and paled even further. The pain from her side had her growing faint. Then, she felt the van slow even more and turn once again, this time to drive slowly up a rutted path, rocking from side to side. Brady's hands tightened on hers and she heard him muttering something, not quite catching what he was saying.

The van stopped and she felt the movement as the two men dropped down out of it, an argument ensuing. The door slid open and she felt Brady pulled from the seat and then hands reached to pull her out. She dropped to her knees, her bound hands finding her side as pain shot through it before a hand dragged her to her feet and then shoved her over rough ground. Fynn was barely able to keep to her feet before she was shoved forward, losing her balance and falling down. She hit the packed dirt and lay still, not hearing the door pulled closed on creaky hinges and a lock snapped closed. Her eyes shuts as waves of pain rocked through her body and she felt the nausea beginning. Please, Lord, don't let me be sick. I can't handle that. Please, Lord. Her eyes closed as she fought against the nausea and pain and then, she lost consciousness, not hearing the man return and stare down at her before he roughly shoved her over to her back with a booted foot and then reach to cut through the ropes binding her. He shrugged. It's wasn't his worry that she didn't stay awake. He had been tasked with finding her and bringing her here. His work was finished.

Brady tilted his head, listening as Fynn was moved away, and then began to fight the hand holding him, trying to get to her. A blow to his jaw sent him to the ground, his vision whirling in front of him as black spots danced in it. He felt hands dragging him up and across the ground, unable to get his feet working before he too was shoved down some stairs, hitting his hands and knees. A hand on the back of his neck kept him still before he was dragged to his knees, his bonds cut and then a shove forward on his back sending him down to his hands and knees again. He waited, hearing the muffled sounds around him, knowing that the door had closed as the light vanished and he heard the loud snick of a lock closing.

He finally reached for the blindfold, dragging it from his head, blinking in the half light that was gradually growing dimmer. Brady stood, his hand reaching to the rough dirt wall to steady himself. A root cellar? He turned abruptly, his head spinning as he did so, and he made his way up the ramshackle stairs, his foot catching on the broken step near the top, and he shoved at the door and then pulled at it, finally giving up and turning around, one hand resting on it, the other rubbing at his face. Fynn? Where are you? Are you okay? Please, Lord, save my lady for me. I don't know who, but you do.

Two days had passed since they had been taken. Food and water had been brought to each one, the man silent as he did so, his face covered so they couldn't identify him. They were given only so long to eat before he returned, gathering up what they hadn't and taking the water bottles with them. Brady sank back against the floor that afternoon, thoughts whirling through his mind. Somehow, he had to get free, to get to Fynn. He had searched for a weapon, finding none in the root cellar, just as he had thought. He had pulled and pried at the door without success. His head tilting, he heard footsteps sounding across the ground and the door flew open. The man beckoned him up. Brady refused, knowing this might be his only chance to escape. He fought with the man, finally managing to knock him down, and running for the stairs and up. He paused, his eyes searching, not seeing the second man until he was tackled and taken down.

A booted foot hit his face as he was going down and he tumbled over and over before he lay still, face down, arms spread out above his head. The men broke out into an argument, each blaming the other for what had happened before the first man reached to flip Brady to his back and then grabbed his wrists, dragging him away from the root cellar and towards the storm cellar that Fynn was captive in. They needed him to take care of her, they had decided, knowing that he was a paramedic. They had brought in supplies for him.

The argument grew louder and louder after Brady was dumped on the packed dirt among the debris that littered it and the men had taken themselves back outside. There was a sudden pop and the second man stared in shock at the first man, a hand raising to his chest before he fell backwards and lay still. The first man stared down at him dispassionately before he looked around and then dragged him to the abandoned barn and dumped his body there. He didn't think he would be found for days. There would be nothing to connect them, he thought. Both of them were from out of town.

Brady roused during the night, laying still, hearing the rustle of the night critters, the call of the night birds and insects and then shifted, a hand going to his face. It hurt. He wiggled his jaw. At least, it's not broken. That's a good thing, isn't it, Lord? He rolled to his side, frowning, before he crawled towards the soft sounds he heard. A hand found a body and he felt for the face. Fynn, he thought. You're here. You're alive. He couldn't assess her, he realized, not in the dark. He sighed before he stretched out near her, a hand on hers, not finding that she even stirred or roused when he did so. This is not good, he thought. He reached to feel her face, finding it burning hot and dry. Oh, Fynn, his heart cried. I need to get you out of here, but I can't. His own head pounding as he laid it back down, his eyes closed and he slept. Neither roused in the early morning as the door opened and the man stood there.

Dropping the food, he stood over them before he spun and ran up the stairs, heading for his ramshackle rusty truck and speeding away as fast as he could. He would find supplies, he thought. That paramedic could do his job then, fix her up and have her ready when his boss appeared late that afternoon. He knew his own life was on the line if they were awake when that happened.

Chapter 39

Brady roused slightly late that afternoon as he felt hands on him before he was raised carefully to his feet and directed up the stairs, the same hands holding him upright. He vaguely remembered stating that he was sick, that he had told his father he didn't feel well and didn't want to go to school. His heart clenched at the thought. That had been the last words he had said to his father that day. His father had laughed, felt his head, and agreed that he could stay home, that he was sick.

Brady roused again as he felt hands pulling him from the vehicle, protesting at being awakened again before he felt what he thought was a bed under him. He roused later as he felt a hand on his wrist and jerked, his eyes springing open to find Anna watching him.

He had to clear his throat before he could speak, his voice husky. "Anna? Where am I?"

"In our infirmary. Doc's been around. Here. I have some broth for you and some cool water. Drink both." Anna helped hold the cup to his mouth, his hands too shaky to do it on his own. She watched as his head went back on the pillow and he slept, this time just sleep. Pulling the light blanket up on him, her hand rested on his head as she prayed for him, her head turning to watch the door, knowing she had to go find out how Fynn was.

Doc watched Fynn closely before he felt Anna's arm around him. Quiet words about the two and then Doc walked away, heading to find Will and Barnabas.

Dallas studied Brady, knowing him well enough to know he had given all the information that he could.

"The two men? Can you describe them?"

Brady shook his head and regretted it. "Not really. I think you'd get a better picture off the security feed in the hospital.""

"I understand Branigan did just that. Now, Fynn? How is she?"

Brady shrugged. "I have no idea." He was on his feet, heading for the conference room before Dallas could stop him.

Dallas sighed, looked down at the signed statement and tucked it away in his locked briefcase. He studied the piles of courier envelopes before reaching for the first one. Emma, what have you sent? He was soon lost in his work, not seeing Alice appear in the doorway until she spoke.

Alice finally walked away, heading for her car and home. It had been a long day, she thought. Dallas is deep into the investigation. She thought through the scenario that they had found, including the body. She didn't think the couple knew about that. That was something for Dallas or Will to discuss with them.

Dallas stood watching Brady, seeing his concentration on Farr, was it? He walked towards Breck, who stood studying the map on the wall, Darby beside him.

"Breck? Is that really Fynn's brother?"

Breck nodded, his concentration not really on Dallas. "It is. Fynn doesn't know that he's here, I don't think. Brady's not too sure of how to approach him."

"I can see that. Have you talked with him at all?"

Breck finally turned. "I have and so has Will. It's not pretty how he's been raised or not raised. We suspect he was taken because of their parents. And we can't reach their parents at all. Eric has been in contact with his. Apparently, they have not come home at all. And that is puzzling to them. They never don't come home from vacation."

"I see. Do we know where they were?"

Breck nodded. "We do. Barnabas has sent Brendon and Brandon out to Saskatoon to look into it. Barnabas has talked to the police chief out there as has Will."

"Okay. Listen, I have to run. I have their statements so they are free to talk." He looked around. "Where's Fynn?"

"Back in the infirmary. She's still really sick, Doc says, and shouldn't have been up."

"Okay, then. I know you all have been working hard. Send me anything you have that might help."

Breck grinned as Darby appeared back beside him, a file box in his hand. "This is what we have. Burnie has sorted through it with Brennen and put it into order for you, he says."

Dallas stared at the box. "Thanks, I think. Catch you later."

Brady finally approached Farr, who stood, feeling lost and lonely, watching the activity and how well the men worked together. He had watched as well as the young wives had come and gone, bringing food, including him. He had liked that they all were friends. That was what he had been missing his whole life, he decided. He needed to change that. Once he made sure Fynn was on her feet and well again, he would leave. He was too dangerous to be around her.

"Don't you leave her."

Farr spun at the harsh words from beside him and stared up at Brady. "I'm sorry?"

"I said, don't leave your sister. I won't let her grieve for you again."

"You must be Brady."

"I am. And you are Farr. You look like your sister. I've seen you around town. I didn't know Fynn had a brother here in town. In fact, Fynn had forgotten you."

"And I had forgotten her. We were torn apart and because of our parents." Anger and bitterness coloured Farr's words. "Look, you need to be sitting down. You're going to fall over if you don't."

Brady nodded, fatigue weighing even that down. "I do. Sit with me." He looked up with a word of thanks as Cadee handed him a mug of coffee. "Thanks, Cadee."

She hugged him and then turned away quickly, blinking back the tears that threatened. Her heard raised in prayer for her friends. Lord, heal them. They need that. So does Farr. We need to bring him into our group, but I am not sure we can.

Chapter 40

A week later, Fynn moved around her apartment, Eric leaning against the kitchen doorframe watching her. She has been too quiet, he thought. He had talked to Dallas, passing on information he had been handed by an informant in his town. Dallas had looked at it, nodded, and thanked him, stating that would help to tie up some of the loose ends. And there were many, he had been warned.

"Fynn?" When she didn't respond, he walked directly into her path and made her.

Fynn glared at her cousin and went to move around him, his hand on her wrist stopping her. He felt her flinch as he did that and dropped his hand. She had more healing to do than he had thought.

"Eric? Have they told you anything? I feel like I am walking around, something hanging over my head ready to drop on me and kill me. Brady feels the same way." Before he could respond, he heard her phone and saw her pale.

"Fynn?"

"That's Dad's ringtone. He hasn't call me in months. Why now?"

"He hasn't? Longer than they have been away?"

She nodded. "Yes. Like in six months and that was only an order that I had to be at a dinner they were giving. I couldn't go. I was on call that night and had been called out to another district. He doesn't understand."

"No and he should. It's been explained to him enough times. You know that body Brady found?"

"Yes, that one. I know. It's tied to here somehow. Dallas said he was an employer of the couple they are looking at. He can't say much, he said, other than that the investigation is moving rapidly. He's worried about Farr."

"Farr, yes. Have you and he talked?"

Fynn nodded, tears momentarily blinding her. "We have. Eric, it was too cruel. I lost a brother growing up, he a sister. I know you've stepped in but it's not the same.'

Eric reached to hug her, his eyes on the door as it opened and Brady appeared, still in his uniform. "I know, Fynn. That I know. I did the best I could as a cousin."

She nodded, hearing Brady's boots hit the tray she left by the door for them. "Brady's here. He shouldn't be. He's not to be done work yet."

"Fynn?" Brady's hands reached to turn her, his eyes looking up at Eric, who nodded. "I had to come. Will asked me to."

"Brady? Why? I don't like this. You're too sober." She reaching to hug him. "Who is it? Who's dead? Please, not Farr. Not Eric's people."

"No, it's not them." An arm around her, he directed her to the couch, holding her close to him when they were seated. A prayer rose in his heart, knowing he would hurt the one that he loved and that he had no choice. "It's your parents."

"My parents? What about other?" She leaned back, studying his face, seeing the sorrow there. "They're dead?"

"I'm sorry. Brendon and Brandon called Barnabas, who found me. I don't have all the details, but they told him that it was a drive by shooting."

"Deliberate. They were followed and then taken out, as they say." She sat in silence, in shock, before she looked at Eric. "You knew?"

"Not for sure. Barnabas had asked me to be with you until he could spring Brady to come home."

She nodded and rose, disappearing, her bedroom door closing quietly behind her. "This is it, isn't it, Lord? Now, I'll never know how to reach them or why they were so distant. I think it has to do with Farr, but I'm not sure. Please, dear Lord, Farr and I will need You. Brady is here, but he didn't know my parents. They refused to meet him." She frowned before she was running for Brady, finding him standing waiting for her, his arms open to sweep her to his heart.

"Brady, they didn't want to meet you. How come?"

"I never knew that. Did you, Eric?"

Eric shrugged. "I just thought it was them being them. They really didn't care what Fynn do or who she hung around with. I don't know that they met many of your friends."

"They didn't. Now, how does all this tie to here? I don't remember them ever talking about this town."

"Dallas is looking into that. He had a lead he was following." Eric's eyes dropped for a moment before he raised them. "I need to run, Fynn. I am so sorry." He reached to hug his cousin and then set her back from him, his hands on her shoulders before he looked up at Brady and nodded, turning to walk away, sorrow and yes anger in his heart towards his aunt and uncle. A sudden thought had him stopping in his tracks before he ran down the stairs towards his vehicle and headed for Dallas. Dallas just stared at him before he nodded, having had the same thoughts.

Chapter 41

Another week had passed. Fynn was growing stronger, but still angered by what had happened to her. She knew she needed to let it go but was having difficulty with that very deed. Brady had talked to her. Buckley had talked to her. Berneen had finally pulled her aside one day, sat her down, went through the Scriptures with her and then prayed with her, leaving her with her thoughts and a hug. She didn't know where Farr stood with God and that bothered her. He had been around, staying in the building as he was, but not as much as she would have liked. They had talked some, but he had become distant and withdrawn. She really didn't know how to deal with that.

Barnabas found her as she stood, staring out of the lobby windows, wanting desperately to be outside but not sure if it was even safe. He shook his head after a moment and approached her.

"Fynn? Do you have some time? The building is at the point that they need some more input from you."

"It is? How did it get ahead that fast?"

Barnabas laughed. "Because it's for you. Once the contractor heard who it was, he put everyone on it. He said you had helped a family friend solve a death years ago."

"I did? I have worked on so many. I'm tired of that, Barnabas. Burnt out. Beaten down."

He nodded, sympathy on his face. "Of course, you are. You've done this for so many years. You pushed your way through, trying to please your parents. You never had a chance to be a teenager, a young lady. Brady realizes that, you know. That's why he's not pushing you any harder than he is. It's the rest of us that want to see you two settle down together."

Fynn blinked at him, before she hugged him. "Thank you. Very few people get that. Are we safe to go?"

"We are. I spoke with Dallas. Alice is here to provide an escort for us. Our security team has a car as well to follow us."

"Wow! Not taking any chances, are you?" Fynn felt life beginning to stir within her once more.

She stood in what would be her office, looking around, knowing she would need to make decisions as to what she wanted for decor and furnishings. Just for the moment, though, she paused, thankful for the friends that Brady had brought into her life and thankful that God had spared her life.

She walked back through the building, the contractor approaching her. Lost in their conversation, Fynn didn't see Barnabas and Brady approaching her, a grin on Brady's face as he saw her excitement. She squealed as his arms surrounded her from behind.

"Happy, love?"

She nodded, a mouthed word of thanks to Barnabas. "I am. This is so me. What I have dreamed about. Does God let us fulfill dreams this way?"

The contractor grinned at her. "He does. He uses people like me to do that. That happiness in your voice? It wasn't there when we spoke last week. It is today. That gives me all the thanks I need. We'll be speaking again, Fynn."

Fynn watched as he walked away before she turned to Barnabas. "Okay, spill. You have news."

Brady began to laugh at the comical look that crossed his friend's face. "You don't get away with much with her, my friend."

"That I can see. You have a handful there, Brady." He grinned at her squeal of outrage. "I do have word. Dallas is meeting us after supper at the building. He can't make it before. Right now, how be we head home? I hear tell Anna and the other ladies have arranged a potluck."

"They have? They didn't tell me. I don't have anything to bring."

"Fynn." When she looked up at him, Brady just smiled. "You don't need to. There will be plenty and you will have opportunities in the future to share."

She shrugged. "It's just not right. That's all I can say. What does he want?"

"That he didn't say. Just asked if you two would be around. I promised him that I would make sure you were."

"Planning our lives, are you?" She walked away, leaving Brady laughing, Barnabas staring after her.

"Did she just do that?"

"She did. She's right. It sounds as if you were planning our lives." Brady ran to catch up with her, an arm around her. "Okay, love?"

She nodded. "Getting there. I'm angry, Brady, and have told God that. I have yelled at Him, been repentant, sobbed out my feelings, been as emotional as I ever have been. I want this over. We need to make plans."

"I know." He looked back as Barnabas walked towards them. "How about we set a date? We can announce it tonight."

"Really? We can do that?" She reached to hug him, holding him tight before she stepped back. "Then, two weeks from Saturday. Buckley stopped me this morning, questioned if we had set a day, and told me that he was free that day, would it do?"

Brady shouted with laughter, unable to resist at the smirk she sent his way, simply shaking his head at Barnabas.

Brady stood after their meal, his hands on Fynn's shoulders, as he waited for his friends to notice. Quiet finally moved through the room as their eyes watched him and then dropped to Fynn.

"We have an announcement to make, my friends." Brady's eyes dropped to the copper hair in front of him. Thank you, Lord, that You have sent Fynn into my life. We're still in for a rough ride, but You are there. She has brought joy and fun into my life in a way that I didn't know I missed. "We have set a day. Buckley, I understand you are free two weeks from Saturday. Will that do?"

Buckley shouted with laughter as his words came back to him. "It will and I am. Congratulations, you two." His eyes moved past the couple to rest on Dallas, who stood, Alice and Will with him, just inside the doorway. This is not good, he thought. Not at all.

Chapter 42

Dallas shook his head. This was always the difficult part, so near the conclusion of the investigation but so dangerous for the victims. And that was what they were, victims. He searched and saw Farr sitting beside Blair, deep in conversation. He looked down as he felt something touch his hand and then reached to pet Kade, Bradon's Australian Shepherd.

"Dallas? You have what you need to give an update?" Will's voice was quiet.

"I do. I needed both of you here as you have information to pass on. Alice, I haven't heard. Did they identify the body Brady found?"

"They did. It was a family member to the couple. From what I understand, he was sent up there to take out Fynn. How he got put in the woods, we don't know, but we suspect her father did the deed."

"That makes cruel sense, you know." Dallas walked towards the young couple, Fynn's eyes meeting his, the sparkle of happiness fading a bit.

"Dallas. Alice. You're here. You need to hear our news." Fynn struggled for a moment, finding her happiness once more. "We've set a date and you both need to come."

"You have? You hadn't the last time we spoke." Alice slipped into a chair beside Fynn. They were become close friends, sharing a faith but also a connection through their occupations.

"We have. Buckley told me he was free two weeks from Saturday. Will this all be wrapped up by then?"

Dallas grinned at her for a moment, knowing exactly what she was doing, pushing him to clear it all off his desk in two weeks. "We will do our best. We have some updates to give you and the rest. Do you have time now? You're finished your meal?"

"We have except to clear the remains away. And that won't take long." She was on her feet, moving away from them, a hand to her side for a moment as the healing muscles pulled.

"Does she ever stop?"

"Sometimes but not for long." Brady turned to face Dallas. "Is it good news you have to share?"

"To some extent."

Dallas finally stood, his eyes wandering over each face that was there, lingering on Farr as he sat beside Fynn, who was sandwiched between Brady and himself. He nodded. They will take care of her. Eric sat beside Farr, his eyes on his cousins, a desperation in his heart that it would be over for them and they could all heal. Yes, he thought, even me, Lord, and my parents. We need to heal as well, and only You can provide that.

Dallas cleared his through, his thoughts scrambled for a moment, so unlike him. He hated this part of it, when he had most of the information to share, but not the culprits. They had gone underground and the search was on. Information was trickling in to the detachment in a steady stream, picking up more and more as each hour went by. The street people knew Brady. They knew he worked for the Foundation and that the Foundation had and would provide for them, what they needed and sometimes even what they wished for.

Will watched as well, his focus on Farr, a frown on his face. Something was off about him that night, he thought, but what? What did they really know about him, other than what he had told them? He spoke quietly to Alice, who nodded.

"I looked into him, Will. He's clear. I don't know what is going on tonight, but he's not involved in her kidnapping. He hasn't had contact with the men we've picked up. They deny knowing him, but I am sure that they have to."

"I'm sure that they do."

Dallas began to speak, drawing all eyes to him.

"Fynn. Brady. Farr. First, Fynn and Farr, your parents. They were targeted, that has been determined by the police in Saskatoon. They didn't have a chance. We haven't been able to determine if they were there for any other reason than what they said, a holiday. The authorities are just waiting for word from you two as to where to return their remains.'

Fynn and Farr exchanged glances before Fynn spoke. "As far as I am concerned, they can be buried out there. I have no reason to visit their graves. They made sure of that." She sighed in the silence. "I know. That's not the attitude I should have. I'm sorry. They had shown all my life that I was an encumbrance to them, a nuisance. No matter what I did, I couldn't reach them."

Benen spoke up. "We understand, Fynn, probably better than you think. We have seen the change in you since you moved here. We stand with you in your decision. Farr?"

Farr shrugged. "I don't remember them all that well. For me to go to their grave? It would be going to a stranger's grave. So, I guess I would agree with Fynn."

"Okay, that's about what I thought you'd say. I'll relay that to the authorities out there. Any expenses I have been told that are not met by their insurances will be picked up by the Foundation. Is that correct, Barnabas?"

"It is, Dallas. It's what we do, Fynn, Farr. We take care of our family and both of you are that." Barnabas nodded at the gratitude on Brady's face.

"Brady, we need to go back to that body you found. It was the son of the couple we are looking for. Farr, did you know that they had a son?"

Farr looked surprised and then shook his head. "No, I didn't and I should have. Where was he?"

"Away at boarding school and camps for all his life, until he became an adult. Then, they groomed him to fit into their business. And by grooming, it was not good. He became their exterminator, to be in one way. Fynn, he was there to kill you. Did you know that?"

Fynn paled. "No, but is he the one that I felt watching me, who went through my home and office?"

Dallas shook his head. "He's the one who had been watching you, but not the one who went through your home and office. I'm sorry. We have confirmation that your father was the one. He was looking for any evidence you might have against him and your mother."

Fynn nodded, having already reached that conclusion. "That doesn't surprise me at all. He used to search my room every day and I know he tried to get into my locker at school. Why?"

"He was involved in white collar crime. He was an accountant, was he not? He used to launder money for the mob, and the couple who took you, Farr, were part of it. They apparently took you to keep him silent, only it didn't work. He really didn't care if you lived or died. I'm sorry. I wish both of you had had better lives."

Farr shrugged. "It is what it is. God protected us, gave us experiences we can use to help others. What else do you have?"

"We have determined, with the help of the police in your hometown, that your father is the one who murdered him. He made arrangements to meet him there. You weren't to be the one called in, Fynn. He had hoped that the body would never be discovered. This we have determined from detailed notes found in his safe."

"That safe!" Fynn leaned forward. "What all was in it? Or can you tell me?"

"I can give only generalities. It is part of the investigation that won't be released yet. There were financial records, thousands of dollars in cash, and a safety deposit box key. That box has been turned over to the authorities. They may be contacting you."

She shrugged. "I don't know anything about it." She looked up at Brady for a moment, finding his trust and confidence in her showing on his face. "Farr wouldn't either, would he?"

Farr was shaking his head. "No. And I know nothing about the people who raised me. Like Fynn, I was barely tolerated,"

"That's the word we have. Now, your kidnappers. We have the one in custody who took you the first time and then from the hospital. He is not talking but won't make bail as yet. He is facing murder and kidnapping charges relating to your case but he is a person of interest in numerous others."

"Murder?" Brady watched as Fynn's face paled before he spoke again. "Who did he murder?"

"The second kidnappers. We found his body in the barn."

Fynn's emotions overwhelmed her for a moment and she turned her face into Brady. "How sad! I mean, they did that to us and likely others, but that is no way to end your life."

"We understand that, Fynn. We really do." Dallas paused, taking the bottle of water Berneen handed him as she moved around the room with Cadee and Ennis, handing out beverages to all of them.

"Where do we stand now, Dallas? Do you have the couple in custody?" Farr was anxious to hear that they were. He had been contacted by a friend, who had indicated that his parents or so-called parents were looking for him, and that he had been told it was not for his good. In fact his friend had asked him to leave town, his very life depended on it.

"No, we haven't yet, Farr. We are going to ask that you and Fynn not leave the building or the immediate surrounding area." He held up a hand at Fynn's protest. "We know, Fynn. We know. You don't want to be restricted in that way but we need to. Sources on the street have told us that there are contracts out on both of you and on Brady as well. Brady, Will took the liberty of talking to your supervisor. For now, you're off on sick leave."

Brady nodded, already having come to that conclusion. "I don't need to go off on sick leave. I spoke with him earlier today, I think after Will did. I have taken a leave of absence for now, which is fine. It's an agreement we all have with our employers."

Dallas was not surprised, having already been warned by Barnabas how the men were employed. "That's good. I can't stress enough that you three stay safe. They are still in the area. That much we know." He turned to Ennis. "Ennis, how did you come up with that farm?"

Ennis shrugged, her eyes on Barnabas. "I have no idea. God, I guess. We used to come to it when we were teenagers. Drawn to the haunted farm. Barnabas used to do the same. When I saw him pointing to where the van went over the bluffs, I remembered how close it was. It was just too convenient."

"Very convenient, I would say. I am just so thankful that Brady and Fynn weren't in it. We would not be having this conversation if they had been."

Chapter 43

Two weeks later, on the Friday night, Fynn stood in a room in the church building, her eyes on her brother as he paced.

"Farr? What's wrong?"

He turned, hesitated, and then came to hug her, standing back with his hands resting on her upper arms. "I'm sorry we lost all this years, Fynn. You are a beautiful, talented, Godly woman I would have loved to have grown up with."

"Thank you. God had a reason, Farr, that we don't know about. We may never here on earth. I am taking my experiences and putting them to use as a volunteer. My building is almost ready and I can start my collections and studies. I already have the schools approaching me about teaching from there."

"That's great." His eyes lifted to the door. "Brady's a great guy. He loves you deeply."

"I know, just as I do him. Now, you need to find someone." She caught the grin he tried to hide. "Let me guess. Alice."

His grin broadened. "Alice but we won't date, not yet. Not until this is done."

"I am so glad, Farr. She's a wonderful friend." She turned as she heard footstep.

Doc stood there, his heart happy for his young friends, but concern weighed him down. This wasn't over, not by a long shot. Precautions were being taken, but it was safe to say that until the couple were in custody, Fynn, Brady and Farr were not safe.

"We're ready for you, Fynn. Farr, you're the one escorting her to Brady?"

Farr grinned, his likeness to his sister evident. "I am. Let's go, Fynn. By this time tomorrow, it will be over and you'll be with the love of your life."

"I like that thought, mister." Fynn grew lighthearted, determined to set the trouble aside for the next few days. She didn't tell Farr that she and Brady were planning on disappearing for a few days, not going too far, but to a cottage of some friends of Doc's. They hoped to avoid being spotted.

The next afternoon, Brady turned from where he stood beside Blair, his eyes on his bride, amazed that the beautiful lady was his. Buckley watched the couple, amusement lurking in his eyes as he remembered how Fynn had asked the question Brady should have. They will never live that down, now will they, Lord?

A week later, Fynn moved through Brady's apartment, settling in, her hands reaching to move things around to add things of her own. Not that she had a lot, she thought. Most of what she had belonged in her office at her building. And that Brady had promised to help her with tomorrow. She understand clearly that they would have security with them, that the couple still had not been found. That worried her. She knew Brady was anxious to get back to work, but won't go, not wanting to put his fellow workers at risk.

Brady stood for a moment, his hand behind his back holding the peach coloured roses that Benen had brought him at his request. He was content, he thought. Thank you, Lord, for your protection over the past week. Fynn needed that, to feel she was safe and just be normal.

Fynn turned, her eyes on Brady. "What are you hiding behind your back?" Her face lit up as she saw the roses. Brady groaned to himself, realizing he had missed out on something. He should have been doing this all along.

The next morning, they headed for her office, his truck filled with boxes, Blair and Bradon following with another truckload. She had apologized but the men had grinned at her, saying it was nothing and just where did she want her things?

Fynn wandered her building, smelling the freshness of the paint and stain, the newness of it. She had a lot to be grateful, she thought.

Brady finally tracked her down, watching as she sat at her desk, her hands flat on the top, her head turning as she studied the room.

"Get everything settled the way you want?"

She gave a quick grin. "Pretty much. Things will get moved around, but you have to work in an office or a building to know the bones and how it feels before you can really settle in. Are we ready to go?"

"We are. Blair and Bradon have gone. Just the security team waiting for us." He paused as he heard a door open and close. "They weren't planning on coming in."

Fynn froze before she rose and headed for the door. "I don't like this." Her walk towards the front of the building halted suddenly as she stared at the couple standing in front of her. "Well, well, well. Who do we have here?"

The man sneered at her, a weapon held up and pointing towards Brady. "You know who it is. You two are coming with us. You've cost us plenty."

"Brady, I would like you to meet Duane and Eva Woolley. Friends or so-called friends of my parents. But you weren't really, now were you?"

"Shut up and move this way." The weapon wavered between the two of them.

"I don't think so, Duane." Fynn had seen the door open silently and close behind Dallas, Alice and some other officers. "We're not going anywhere. But you can explain something. Why did you kidnap Farr?"

"It wasn't supposed to be Farr. It was supposed to be you. The man who took him couldn't find you. He took your brother instead." Eva sneered at her in turn. "Let's just say, he'll never make that mistake again."

Fynn paled even as she shifted closer to Brady. "You killed him?"

"Not us, but it happened. He was working for too many bosses and that screwup was the last straw. Now, walk this way. We're going to go for a nice little drive, end up near the quarry, take you two for a little stroll. Only you won't be coming back."

Eva gave a scream as her wrist was caught and pulled behind her, the snap of handcuffs loud in the air. Duane made to turn, his weapon on Brady as he felt a weapon jab his back.

"I would drop that, if I were you. Duane Woolley. You are under arrest for kidnapping, attempted murder, murder, and whatever else we can come up with."

"I want my lawyer." Duane's whine sounded loud in the silence.

"And you will have. Okay, off you go with my friends here. They'll take you two for a nice little car ride of your own to a nice large building with cells in them. We have a lot of information on you two. Today? That's the icing on the cake." He watched as the pair were led away before he turned to Fynn and Brady.

"You two okay?"

Fynn have a huge breath. "We are, finally. This is it? They're the last ones?"

"We believe so. I'll have to ask you two to stay safe for another few days, but this should wrap it up. I'm glad for you two and for Farr."

"And for Alice." Fynn grinned at Alice who looked surprised before she too grinned.

"Alice?"

Brady began to laugh, having heard from Fynn Farr's story. "Now that this is over, Farr and Alice can begin dating. Another wonderful couple, I must say." He looked down at Fynn with a smile, crooked his arm and then led her away when she looped her arm through his.

Dallas stood and watched them, a bit of shock on his face causing Alice to laugh. He twisted his head to watch her. "You and Farr?"

"Me and Farr. Now, let's blow this joint, as my Dad would say. Fynn wants to lock up. They have some celebrating to do."

"That they do. By the grace of God, they do."

Epilogue

Brady was on a hunt through Fynn's building, not finding her. He paused, his hand on his head before he nodded, and headed out the back door, towards the flower beds she had worked up and planted with multiple kinds of perennials. He could hear the bees from the hives a beekeeper had been glad to bring over.

He stood, his eyes on her as she knelt on the ground, bent over looking at something before he walked towards her, kneeling beside her.

"What are we watching, love?"

She looked up, a grin on her face. "The ants. They are such busy creatures. God made them. He even directs us to consider them, to watch how them work and store away for winter. It struck me as I was watching them that is what I need to do. I need to store His words away in my heart. I didn't have enough when I needed them."

"You had the ones He wanted you to have and He made sure you had just the right amount." His hand took her to pull her to her feet before he led her to the arbour she had wanted. "This is nice. But going back to your thoughts, He planned for all this."

Fynn's head went down on Brady's shoulder. "He did. It has been, what two months? It feels like forever and yet still like yesterday. The guys and the ladies have been so gracious."

Brady nodded. "It's who they are. I know we're not done, not by a long shot, not with our adventures as we term them. I had a long talk with Abe the other day, about how he coped."

"They have quite the story, don't they? Married, torn apart by greed with Abe thinking she didn't want him and Emma thinking he was dead. And all their guys and so many of their friends." She looked up at Brady. "God protects us. But He also heals. I have turned so much to the story of the woman who touched Christ's garment and find peace."

"I also do but I also find peace in knowing that God is the God who heals us. He takes our brokenness and brings something new and refined from it."

"That he does." Fynn sighed, content for the moment. "Brady, thank you for being who you are."

"And you as well, love."

They finally rose as twilight was descending, Brady locking up her building before wrapping her in his arms and kissing her. She was the helpmeet God had planned for him. *Lord, help me to be worthy of the woman whose price is far above rubies. I know there will be times I screw up but help us to be open with one another and build the marriage You have planned for us.*

Dear Readers:

Thank you for once more picking up one of my novels, this time the story of Brady and his Fynn. I had fun with this one, insects fascinating me for years. Back in the 1960's my father worked for a lumber company, building homes and cottages. There were many times he would bring something home to show my sister and myself, whether it was a leaf in the fall or an insect. One time he even brought us a pony for Christmas.

Forensics entomology fascinates me, being able to determine the age of eggs, larvae and insects to help solve a crime. Perhaps, if I had chosen differently, I might have done that. Being a paramedic is a difficult work. I have had exposure to them with my Mom's sudden passing and with my Dad who had health issues. Wonderful people who had a difficult task.

It was not planned that Fynn would have a brother who had disappeared on her. Characters have a way of just walking into the stories, usually dragged in by another one. I call the characters in my books unruly, as they don't let me write the story I planned but take over as soon as I set fingers to the keyboard, take off and as an author friend has said, don't let me have a road map or a GPS unit to know where I'm headed. But I love them. Bringing in Abe and Emma brought back beloved characters from the *His Guardians Series*. Their story is the last one in that series, *His Protector*.

God is a God who heals. He does not want us to be broken. I have attempted to show that in Fynn and Farr and even with Brady. They had to learn to trust Him in a way that we don't think we can. A favourite passage of Scripture is the woman with the issue, who touched just the hem of Christ's garment. I have used this in another book, *A Touch of His Garment*, involving close friends of Abe and Emma. (Do I like the town of Riverville and its characters much? I do and miss them.)

God bless each one of you. Reach out to touch the hem of the garment. He provides not just physical healing but any healing.

Ronna

Lightning Source UK Ltd.
Milton Keynes UK
UKHW022209060820
367830UK00011B/1325/J